HEART WAVES

Gloria Alvarez

A KISMET® Romance

METEOR PUBLISHING CORPORATION

Bensalem, Pennsylvania

For Dean, who wrote the history
of my heart.

And with thanks to the Gulf Coast
Writers' Retreat: Martha Corson,
Jo Ann Vest and Linda West; and
all the Crescent City Writers.

GLORIA ALVAREZ

Gloria Alvarez was destined to become a writer. As a child, she was surrounded by books—everything from *Mother Goose* to the *Wizard of Oz* to biographies of Queen Elizabeth I. And once she learned to write, there was no stopping her. She wrote poetry, short stories, book reviews and even advertising copy. Now she spends her time writing romantic stories in America's most romantic city, New Orleans, where she lives with her husband and fifteen tropical fish.

PROLOGUE

"Cassidy Sloane!" Peyton Adair groaned as she and Sally Ashton made their way down the narrow corridor of the radio station. "And I thought this buyout couldn't get any worse."

"Peyton, get a hold of yourself!" Sally scolded her friend. "You've known that new management was coming ever since WFKN was put on the auction block."

"But I didn't expect Cass Sloane!" Peyton groaned again. "It gives me chills just to think about it."

"Honey," the older woman said, "we all know Mr. Sloane's reputation. He's a fast track golden boy with a real big perfectionist streak. But he's convinced somebody that he's got what it takes to turn us around."

"A stockholder's dream and a manager's nightmare," Peyton said bleakly, pulling her auburn hair from its loose chignon and shaking it around her shoulders. "He lives and dies by the ratings."

"Don't we all, honey! Don't we all!"

"Yeah," she admitted softly. "How do you stay so calm, Sal?"

Sally shook her head and shrugged, her short salt and pepper hair bouncing. "After twenty-eight years in the business, how else could I be? You don't stay in radio if you can't adapt. If he fires me, well, it wouldn't be the first time I've had to look for work. Though," she added wryly, "the timing couldn't be much worse if he does. Tuition just about wiped us out this semester, and Andy has this bad habit of outgrowing his clothes every couple of months."

Peyton nodded in sympathy. With twins in college and her "surprise child" now a toddler, Sally worked because she had to. Like so many women of the nineties, she couldn't afford to stay home.

"Do you ever get used to it?" Peyton asked. "The waiting, the indecision?"

Sally shook her head. "Nope," she said bluntly.

"Some comfort." Then Peyton voiced the real fear that had been gnawing at her for a month, ever since the news of the radio station's impending sale. "Layoffs plain scare me."

Sally wagged a motherly finger. "You've just been incredibly lucky. For most of us, getting axed is a medal of honor. It means you've got guts."

Sally was right, Peyton reflected. But it didn't make the next few days any easier to face. Her job, her career, and her future were all on the line because the new owners of WFKN had lured Cass Sloane from New York to Columbus, Ohio. He was a hotshot announcer who had moved over to management and proved he could be just as hot there.

The new owners had no doubt promised Sloane carte blanche to monkey with the programming and the people. Rumor had it that he would work no other way. The carefully wrought schedules and personalities that Peyton had built for the past three years were bound to come under his attack. Peyton shivered at the prospect, suddenly cold despite the warm August afternoon.

"It'll be okay," Sally reassured her. She put her arm around Peyton and gave her a quick hug and a dose of her ready advice. "Just do your job today and let tomorrow worry about itself."

But Peyton couldn't follow that simple counsel. She'd always looked ahead, planning, dreaming, working towards a new goal as soon as she'd achieved her previous one. Peyton had always seized control of her own destiny, from the time she was fifteen and had found her first job in radio.

She closed her eyes for a second, and scenes from her youth clicked like a movie reel: Dad coming home from the second shift at the Ford plant, tired and worried because orders were slow and the factory was shutting down; her mother concerned about how to feed and clothe four children; the budget "discussions" that inevitably left both father and mother drained and unhappy. They'd coped by lavishing love where there was no money. But Peyton had grown up sensing that losing a job was one of the worst things that could happen to a person. Layoffs meant insecurity, disappointment, and shattered dreams.

She'd avoided all three during her radio career. She'd molded herself into a team player, willing to take on any responsibility. She worked hard and planned her moves carefully, so that she was never without a new challenge, and more important, never without a steady job.

And her strategy had worked.

Until now. Now she was faced with Cass Sloane and the prospect that for once her best wouldn't be good enough.

ONE

Cassidy Sloane had arrived. And if people had been uncertain before, now they were as edgy as a new razor blade. Peyton sensed the tension from the moment she walked into the tenth floor conference room. A general staff meeting could only mean one thing.

Immediate changes.

They weren't unexpected, of course. A few folks had already found work and resigned. Others had begun packing the personal items from their desks in anticipation.

And Peyton couldn't do anything to quell their mood because, despite her status as program director, she'd been kept in the dark. She'd received exactly one memo from the elusive Mr. Sloane, ordering her to arrange this morning's staff meeting. The note had provided no other clue about what he intended to do with the station.

Peyton spied Sally perched on a window sill and walked over to join her.

"Looks like this is it," Sally said nonchalantly.

"This place is a powder keg," Peyton whispered, looking around at her colleagues with their halfhearted smiles and nervous waves. "I think our illustrious Mr. Sloane is making a big mistake. He should have met with the directors first and worked out a transition plan."

"Not his style."

"Maybe not, but it's still a mistake. Not everyone can be as casual about this as you."

"No need to get snappish," Sally reproved. "I don't *want* to lose my job. But if I do, I have options. So does everybody else."

"You're right." Peyton smiled. "But that's hard to remember in the face of layoffs."

"It'll be okay," Sally said quietly. She reached over and squeezed Peyton's hand briefly, and Peyton realized she was shivering.

A sudden hush fell over the room as a tall man in a dark gray suit strode in. People shifted in their seats to catch a better glimpse of the new general manager. Cass Sloane.

He stood straight and broad shouldered, lean and muscular. His jacket hung in well-tailored lines, the warm, rich color contrasting sharply with his hair, which was a cool blond, almost silver. He wore it short, brushed straight back. His nose was sharp and straight, his jaw decisive. A deep line was etched across his forehead, and its thinner cousins stood watch at the corners of each eye.

His eyes. Peyton notched her chin up and met his gaze as he surveyed his audience. Even from the edge of the room, she could see blue—the steely, unflinching blue of winter.

"I'm Cassidy Sloane," he began without preamble. "I'm here to announce the start of the new WFKN."

His voice! She'd heard him on tape, of course, but

in person he was even better—rich and smooth as heavy cream in coffee. It was the ideal voice for radio.

Or bearing bad news.

Cass spoke again. "Undoubtedly you've been wondering what the future holds. It's simple. Under my leadership, WFKN will be *the* driving force in Columbus, Ohio. We will be number one. I can do it. I've done it in New York and Chicago and Los Angeles. I can do it here. But being number one means change. I don't win ratings wars with contests or gimmicks. *I* win with programming, advertising packages, and visibility, and that kind of growth is painful. It means personnel cuts, program shuffles, doubling up, picking up slack to build a station that meets the bottom line."

There it was—the all-important bottom line. Never mind that the station had been doing quite well in the ratings without any retooling from this east coast thunderbolt. Never mind that he was toying with people's lives, not to mention the community's expectations of what WFKN should be.

But he sure had one heck of a delivery. He was confident to the point of arrogance. Looking around, Peyton saw that her colleagues sat mesmerized by their new leader. They nodded to the cadence of his speech, its steel edge of sureness holding them captive.

"The future holds promise," he continued, loosening his burgundy and gold splashed tie. "This station can be number one again."

Peyton swallowed hard, shuddered slightly. She had to remain objective. Cass Sloane had already lulled many of her colleagues into complaisance; she knew from looking at them that they'd be inclined to accept, without question, any of his proposals. No doubt about it; this man was a personality to be reckoned with. Charisma sliced through his speech, reaching out and riveting everyone's attention. If he could do that on his first day . . .

"I've been reviewing the station's record for several weeks, and I've based my decisions on what I found. For some of you . . . I'm sorry. For others I offer the chance to work on a flagship station. So without further ado . . ." Cass reached into the tooled leather portfolio he carried and withdrew a sheaf of papers. Without comment he distributed them.

Sally took a copy from the engineer in front of her. She scanned it, shook her head and handed it to Peyton. Then she stood up and walked out. And she wasn't alone. Five other announcers and their producers stood and followed her out the door.

Peyton found the eleven o'clock grid on the paper. The name of a well-known syndicated talk show appeared in the slot Sally had practically owned for seven years.

Peyton scanned the sheet again, this time in shock. There was more satellite programming, fewer local initiatives. "On Campus," the program managed exclusively by college interns, was gone. "Top Kid," Peyton's alternative to Saturday cartoons, had been banished to Sunday mornings at seven.

She'd been fighting this kind of homogeneity since she'd arrived four years ago, fighting it with the WFKN family—the balanced group of programs and personalities that *she* had established. And that group had been inching its way up in market share. Cass just had to give it time.

As general manager, he was within his rights to fine tune the programming—but not by completely dismantling everything that made WFKN unique, not to mention the fact that she wasn't even consulted. Peyton looked at the chart a third time. Her name still appeared on the masthead. She balled her hand into a fist and let the nails dig into her palm. She almost wished she'd been let go, too. As program director, she'd have to implement a new schedule that she totally disagreed with.

"Those of you whose names are on the chart should plan to see me today," Cass said. "Check with the station secretary for your appointment. I'll see advertising tomorrow."

He glanced down at the sheet again. "I'll meet with Ms. . . . Adair immediately. My office." He snapped shut the portfolio. "Let's begin our day. We have a lot of work ahead of us to reach number one."

Without waiting for questions, he strode out the door. Peyton followed right behind, leaving her colleagues muttering about the uncertainties of the radio business and the amazing arrogance—and charisma—of Cass Sloane.

She let him stay a few steps ahead of her, using the time to compose herself, to build her arguments. She loved radio, loved how it opened new worlds. As a child, she'd always been amazed that twirling a dial or punching a button could transport her to a rock concert as readily as it could to a night at the opera or a presidential press conference. It was better than television because it let her imagination roam free.

She'd gotten hooked when her father gave her a small clock radio for her tenth birthday. Five years later came her first job typing ad scripts, sweeping and making coffee for a small Detroit station. The manager had liked her attitude. When she graduated from high school, he supplemented her college scholarship with his own money.

Peyton was profoundly grateful and determined to live up to the expectations of the people who'd believed in her. Someday she too would be able to offer young people the same kind of chance she'd had—at her own station where she could program the kind of radio that had touched her life.

She was well on her way, with eight solid years of experience since college. At thirty, she had only one more big step to take: New York, the major market that would prepare her for every aspect of buying and running a radio station.

The sale of WFKN to an undisclosed consortium of buyers, however, was forcing her to rethink her plan. She had expected to stay at 'FKN another couple of years. But after Cass Sloane's performance just now, she might be leaving a lot sooner than that, either by her initiative or his.

She rapped firmly on Cass's door and then opened it without waiting for an invitation.

The complete transformation of the office stunned her. This man didn't waste any time. She barely recognized the place. While Cass's predecessor, now retired, had favored polished oak and silk upholstery, Cass's tastes ran to smoky glass, chrome and black leather. A computer screen glowed brightly from a side table. Only the picture window remained unchanged, framing the skyline from twenty stories up. The room appeared imposing and vital, a high tech office for a high tech man.

But this was Columbus, Ohio, and the style in vogue in New York might very well backfire in America's heartland.

"Ms. Adair, I presume," Cass said smoothly as she shut the door behind her.

"Mr. Sloane," she acknowledged, holding out her hand stiffly.

He shook hands. His grip was warm and firm, his

palms hardened with callouses. And his touch ignited a dangerous flicker of awareness in Peyton.

It caught her by surprise, and she had to remind herself that Cass Sloane was no ordinary general manager. He'd just brutalized half her staff, including her best friend. She'd do well to remember *that*, not some silly little charge of electricity jolting up her arm.

"Come in. Sit down." Cass sat and gestured beside him on the sofa. Peyton took the chair instead and sank back into the cool, smooth leather, inhaling its fragrance. It had the smell of authority.

And so had Cassidy Sloane, with the charm and ego to match. His display a few minutes ago was calculated to enhance all three.

If she had any hope of gaining his respect, she'd have to compete on his level. A team player wouldn't cut it with Cass Sloane. "I think you made a serious error," she said deliberately.

"Only one?" His tone was faintly sardonic, and it annoyed Peyton.

"Several, as a matter of fact. Starting with Sally Ashton."

"The overnight jock?" Cass waved his hand in dismissal. "There's no revenue in overnights. Local talent adds too much to the bottom line."

"She's been number one for years!" Peyton protested vehemently. "And she has a family to support!"

"If she's been number one, she'll find work. I'm sure you'll provide an excellent reference. Any other complaints?"

She squared her shoulders and dangled the new program chart by a corner. "This. Our ratings have been steadily improving with the old schedule. *My* schedule. The market's not ready for this lineup. It's certainly not WFKN!"

"Maybe not as you know it. But the station hasn't been producing nearly enough listeners or revenues. It's time for changes. *My* changes."

She tilted her head and looked him straight in the eye. *Don't back down*, she told herself. *If you let him run roughshod over you now, he'll never stop. He's just the sort to take advantage that way.*

"So why am I still here?" Peyton demanded. "You disagree with my personnel and programming decisions, and with the way you work as general manager, you don't need a program director. When do I hit the street?"

The lady had spunk, Cass thought, surprised. Not many people would take him on first thing in the morning. And from all reports, Peyton was the cooperative type, the kind who dealt with compromise, not confrontation. He'd been told she managed people well and could handle the day-to-day details he found so confining. That was why she was still here. It was not so his decisions could be challenged.

But it was refreshing in an odd sort of way. So few people stood up to him. Not since Katie . . .

"You're still here," he said abruptly, "because the former management gave you high marks. The station's run efficiently, clocks are on time, and the staff likes you. You still have a lot to learn, because your programming wasn't winning any ratings wars. But I can teach you a thing or two." A devilish light filled his eyes. "And you're right. I don't need a program director. I need a producer for 'On Air Columbus.'"

He knew that announcement would be a bombshell. Cass watched her reaction with interest. She inhaled sharply, the paisley fabric of her dress tightening involuntarily over her breasts. Her gray eyes narrowed, and a slow tide of pink darkened her cheeks. She wasn't pleased, and that was just as well. Keeping people off balance tended to make them sharper.

"Excuse me?" she said angrily. "You've insulted my programming abilities, you've changed the entire schedule without even consulting me, you've dismissed my staff and interns, and now you're demoting me to producer?" She took another deep breath. "Not on your life, Mr. Sloane. I resign."

"I won't accept it." The words were out of his mouth before he had a chance to think. When his instincts reacted this strongly, Cass knew better than to ignore them. Something about Peyton Adair had clicked. Maybe because she stood up to him and defended her beliefs. Maybe because she so obviously cared about the station and her people. Maybe because her face flushed so beautifully when she was angry, her gray eyes flashing like quicksilver.

Whatever the reason, he couldn't let her go yet.

"You don't have a choice," she said as she stood to leave.

"Give me three months, Peyton." He moved effortlessly between her and the door, catching her arm to stop her. "That's all I'm asking."

His fingers sunk into her coppery flesh, and her nervous system short-circuited. She couldn't move; she could barely breathe. The frisson of awareness she'd experienced earlier was replaced with a lightening bolt of sensation, pure, deep and driving.

Good God, what would it be like if he touched her for real?

"Three months," he repeated. "Hang around long enough to get the new 'FKN off the ground. If you decide you don't like working with me, you leave with my blessing. I'll even help you find something in New York, if you want. I have a lot of contacts there. At the very least, staying here for three months will give you a job while you look for something else.''

Deliberately she removed Cass's hand from her arm and stepped out of the circle of his reach. Slowly the sting of his touch receded, and she could consider his proposal objectively.

She'd be crazy to accept, and equally crazy not to. The offer was the best of both worlds, a compromise that she'd have thought Cass incapable of making ten minutes ago. She could keep on working and look for her next position at the same time. It was an ideal arrangement, giving her time to shape up her resumé and dust off her demo tapes—because she had no doubt that she'd have to move on. One touch from Cass Sloane had made sure of that.

She wasn't ready to abandon her goals and dreams— especially not for a self-important egotist like Cass Sloane, no matter what he did to her insides. She still had too much to prove . . . to herself and to her supporters back in Detroit. But those dreams called for experience, she reminded herself. And she could get that experience with Cass—if she didn't let sex appeal and sparks get in her way. The more she thought about it, the more confused the issue became. But she'd learned that in radio you sometimes had to fly on instinct.

''Three months,'' she agreed.

She hoped she wasn't making the biggest mistake of her career.

TWO

"Well, we've got the rest of the staff squared away," Cass said to Peyton two weeks later. "It's time to talk about 'On Air Columbus.'"

They'd spent the past ten days closeted with production teams and advertising account executives. They'd battled over formats, production values, revenue forecasts, and advertising packages.

Slowly Peyton had grown to respect Cass. He was still arrogant, still just shy of tyrannical, but he offered a crystal clear vision of the station's future. He explained his goals brilliantly, and he spoke with eloquence and conviction about WFKN's potential and the concrete methods they had to use to reach number one. Each team had left their meeting hungry for the all-important audience share and the creative ad package they needed to attract new advertisers and increase sales to their regulars.

Like everyone else, Peyton caught the Cass Sloane fever. He'd gotten under her skin, infected her with a new competitive edge. She'd spent a lot of overtime preparing for the day they launched "On Air Columbus."

And too much of that overtime was spent thinking about Cass himself.

Even little things set her mind racing, such as when he'd presented her with a prototype WFKN coffee mug so she could judge how it fit a woman's hands. The only thing she could think of for at least a day was how *he* might fit her hands. One morning he'd brought in a box of chocolates from a new advertiser so the staff could brainstorm ideas for their commercials. Peyton could only conjure an image of Cass and her together, sharing the chocolate in ways her mother would never approve. The picture was not something she cared to advertise over the airwaves.

The constant interaction didn't help. The dozens of times they'd brushed against one another in meetings, accidentally, resulted in an instant of attraction that alarmed as much as fascinated her.

She'd be a fool to think it was mutual, of course. He'd given her no indication that he was interested in anything more than the bottom line—and how she could improve it. But she couldn't help herself. As she'd come to know him, she'd recognized a kindred spirit. He loved radio, loved the challenges and the myriad headaches that running a station brought. If only their approaches weren't so different! If he'd show a little understanding! He'd been furious when he discovered she'd encouraged Sally and the other laid-off staffers to use the station equipment to update their resumés and demo tapes. He'd finally given his grudging approval, but only after she'd accused him of being an automaton, a man without feelings.

She didn't understand why Cass Sloane captivated her imagination—and she couldn't stop herself. He clearly wasn't her type: brash, demanding, a one-man show. But he stayed lodged in her consciousness, keeping her on the edge of anticipation.

"I want real issues that matter to our listeners," Cass said bluntly. "Whether it's Buckeye football or Congressional scandals, the topics have to count. So what have you come up with?"

She took a deep breath and fought to quiet the little knot of excitement that had taken up permanent residence in her stomach. "Your reputation means that national celebrities will be clamoring to talk to you," she began. "But locally you're an unknown. You need to start by establishing your credibility—or offending enough people to get them talking."

"What do you suggest?"

"Brick Villere to start."

Cass frowned. "The writer who claims that the women's movement is responsible for the breakdown of society? That's practically a cliché."

"Of course. The theory's absurd, but everyone's got an opinion! You interview him for half an hour, then open the phones. It's guaranteed to be great radio."

"Can you get him?"

She nodded, a little smug. "His publicist has already called. He's a go."

"What else?"

"Pete Rose, for one. Has the local hero finally reformed? *Is* gambling an addiction? How did prison change him? How he feels about Cooperstown. That sort of thing."

Cass shook his head. "Pete's passé."

Peyton shook her head, too. "Maybe in New York, but not in Ohio. Trust me. Pete Rose will fly."

He frowned again and looked at her closely. Peyton

met his eyes, unflinching, and held her ground. "Pete Rose," she repeated.

Cass gave a sharp nod, as if convinced by her stare-down performance. "If you can get him, I'll talk to him."

They spent the rest of the morning discussing—arguing, really—program ideas: everything from trash-burning power plants to Elvis sightings. He grilled her on every angle, trusted no instinct but his own. As the day wore on, she wondered how she would ever rid herself of all the adrenaline he inspired.

But he *was* efficient. He had a terrific knack for asking the few incisive questions that got straight to the heart of an issue.

By late afternoon they moved on to block programming, catalogues, and advertising strategies. They covered everything: who might sponsor programs on financial planning, child development, and career guidance; whether their listeners would be willing to buy station promotional items like T-shirts, or whether they should be reserved as premiums.

Hammering out ideas with Cass was hard—he interrupted, shot down and added his own ideas. He wasted no energy on careful words or tact. But his face took on an animated glow as they sparred, and Peyton felt flash after flash of kinship with Cass. She couldn't quite catch her breath when he looked at her with that radio-inspired passion. It was too much like her own.

And she was exhausted, utterly drained from the most tumultuous two weeks of her career. "I'm heading home," she announced at seven thirty, a mere eleven hours after they'd begun.

"How about dinner?" Cass stood and rolled his shoulders back, giving her the impression of tightly controlled power. "Those sandwiches at lunch were a poor excuse for food."

"Too tired," she said, too quickly. She needed the safety of home after a whole day of Cass. He incited too many conflicting responses in her—physical and emotional. An evening alone with him would only give her body another chance to overwhelm her good sense. The same good sense she'd ignored when she'd agreed to stay on.

"You have to eat," he pointed out logically. "And Rainer's Würsthaus is right in your neighborhood."

"And how do you know where I live?" she asked, startled. *Good grief, if he knew her address, what else had he chosen to find out? And why?*

"Personnel files, of course. You're in German Village, on . . . Mohawk, I think," Cass said without missing a beat. Then he grinned mischievously. "What do you say? Bremen Brats on me. You've got it coming after today. Though I must say, you've done pretty well for a rookie."

She stared at him in indignation. "If you've seen my personnel file, you know I'm no rookie. I've paid my dues. I earned this job."

"Could be. You served time at a public radio station in Iowa, then six years of commercial experience in North Dakota and Kentucky and Columbus. But this is your first experience putting it all together. In that you're a rookie." He pulled on his suit jacket, straightened his tie and added, "What about dinner?"

Well, she *was* hungry. He owed her for that rookie wisecrack. Buying her dinner ought to about even the score. She agreed.

Once inside the restaurant, Cass wondered what had possessed him to invite Peyton to dinner. It had been another long, tough day in a string of long, tough days.

He needed a solitary bottle. He ought not to be dining with a woman who had taken him on, undaunted by his reputation or his toughness. A woman with hair the color of burnished autumn leaves, eyes that blazed and ripe, full lips that hinted at a softness he hadn't experienced for years.

He took a long draught of his beer. He should respect her professionally; she had the makings of a fine employee, after all. But he ought to dismiss these other images he was seeing—and the emotions she was provoking.

He couldn't. He'd invited her to join him, and now he'd have to deal with every conflicting sense she aroused in him. But good God, he felt more like a tongue-tied teenager than a thirty-eight-year-old radio host with a half a dozen talk shows to his credit. He stared at the menu blindly, unable to concentrate on anything but Peyton's presence across the table, her lithe form settling on the scrubbed wooden bench, her jacket crumpled beside her.

"How do you know Rainer's?" Peyton asked, making conversation.

"Hmm?" He was off balance, out of focus. Recovering, he answered, "I used to come here a lot. I went to Ohio State, you know."

"You're a Buckeye?" Peyton recoiled in mock horror. "I knew there was something really wrong with you. I'm a U of M grad myself."

"Michigan? I have a Wolverine on my staff?" He latched on to the safe subject of alma maters. The rivalry between the two schools was legendary, and their alumni took their loyalties seriously.

"Go, Blue!" Peyton laughed and sipped her lager. Then more seriously she asked, "So you're from Ohio?"

"My wife and I were both from here."

"Your wife?"

"She died several years ago." He could say that now, without too much of the pain that once accompanied those words. Before Peyton could mouth any regrets, he rushed on, "What about you? Where are you from?"

She ignored his question and looked him square in the face, compassion warming her eyes. "I'm sorry, Cass. About your wife." Then without missing a beat, she went on. "I was born and bred in the Motor City. One sister, two brothers, three dogs, and some goldfish. My parents had their hands full with *that* menagerie. Dad worked for Ford, and Mom was a school secretary."

"You came here four years ago?"

She nodded. "Started as promotion director, then got promoted two years ago. Came close to losing it a couple of weeks ago. But you know that." Peyton lifted her mug in a mock toast to the vagaries of radio.

"What about you?" she asked.

"I grew up in Ashville, just south of here. My dad was a farmer. I went to Ohio State and got an internship at WOSU. I've been bouncing around the country ever since."

"Building number one ratings for your shows and your stations."

Cass detected a note of admiration in her voice. It had been too long since he'd inspired anything but fearful respect in an employee. The thought warmed him, but . . .

Not too close, he warned himself. *Never that close again.*

"Why did you leave New York?" she continued. "I thought everybody dreamed of working there."

"Do you?" Cass responded quickly, and Petyon had

the grace to blush. The red stain made her look sweet and vulnerable, and Cass recalled a younger self, still unscarred by tragedy.

That younger man imagined what it would be like to take Peyton's face in his hands and stare down into the slate pool of her eyes. He wondered what it would feel like to test her lips with his, taste the sugar of her skin, bathe in the warmth of her smile.

Not too close, he warned himself again, but the warning died as quickly as the conversation. Cass studied Peyton with the hunger of a starving man. How long had it been since he'd looked at a woman, really looked at her?

God, he wanted her. Wanted to touch her, to blot out the pain and suffering, all the years since Katie . . . Unthinking, he reached across the table and touched Peyton's cheek.

Her face was smooth, still warm and flushed. She felt soft, whole, clean. He stroked the hollow below her cheekbone, marveling at the contrast between the softness of her skin and the calloused pads of his fingers. Her eyes had widened at his touch, glinting with fear and confusion. Regretfully he dropped his hand, but he couldn't disconnect his desire. He still wanted her.

Peyton had entranced him, with her straightforward honesty and love of people. And he was completely wrong to want her.

The waitress brought their sandwiches, and they ate several bites in silence. Cass struggled to bring his errant feelings under control, until finally he could speak without his voice catching. "You didn't answer me," he said softly. "Do you want to work in New York?"

"What radio exec doesn't?" she whispered breathlessly, but whether from sharing her dream or his touch he couldn't tell. "It's the top market in the country. If you can make it there . . ." She lifted a forkful of potato salad to her mouth, then laid it aside, uneaten.

Young and bright and full of ambition, Cass thought. *What a marvelous combination.* Suddenly he felt very old. He'd been those things once. Now he was tired, jaded and hard, with only his career to keep him warm at night.

Peyton must have seen the shadow cross his face, because she asked every gently, "Why did you leave?"

"It was all very complicated," he evaded. No need to tell Peyton how he'd buried the best part of himself with Katie five cold years ago, how he'd built a wall around his heart to protect himself from the terrible pain of her loss, and how he'd finally become just the sort of man Katie had always despised—self-important, arrogant and altogether despicable. He'd come home to try to recover some of his lost humanity.

But it was better to keep it simple than to tell Peyton all of that. "I needed some place quieter, with a slower pace of life. Though it doesn't seem like I've slowed down any these past few days," he added lightly.

"No kidding!" Peyton said, matching his tone. "I thought I worked hard before you came. These last two weeks have been hell."

"Do you mind?"

"Hard work? Not at all. What I mind is stunts like your first day here, cancelling programs and firing people without discussing it with your top staff. I still think you made a serious mistake with Sally Ashton. Not that Sal would come back. She's got too much pride."

"I probably did her a favor," Cass said wryly.

"Maybe. But I'll miss her."

Peyton's eyes burned bright at the thought, and Cass

was again struck by how forthright she was. It was refreshing. Peyton was refreshing.

Off to one side of the restaurant, a German oom pah pah band was setting up, testing their microphones, adjusting the sound, tuning their horns. Somehow in the confusion, Cass had ordered dessert. Now the waitress set an enormous cream puff between them, and Peyton stared hopelessly at it.

"We'll never finish it!" she shouted over the opening strains of the "Beer Barrel Polka." "You'd better plan on eating most of it."

They leaned over the plate, clinking their forks and tearing the pastry shell to scoop out the rich cream. Everything about Peyton's nearness enlivened Cass's sense of her: the loose curls framing her face, her scent of wild jasmine, her tongue tracing a pattern in the custard on her upper lip. He couldn't help himself. Peyton had found her way into his consciousness, making him feel too much too fast.

No! No matter what she might make him feel, he had nothing to offer her. She was on her way up, a shining star. His star had been eclipsed five years ago.

Her foot kept time to the lively folk tune the band was playing. The vibrations snaked their way up his leg—an exquisite torture. He was jumpy, skittish as a colt, and he desperately wanted to kiss Peyton. No matter how wrong, how little he could give her, he wanted her. Here, now, in this room full of strangers and biergarten music, he wanted to slake the thirst he'd built for her.

She's your colleague, a tiny voice reminded him. *Seducing your employee after two weeks is hardly the way to build a new life.*

I'm not seducing her! his inflamed passion roared. *All I want is to kiss her.*

Kisses lead to bigger things, reason spoke again. *You're half mad because this is the first woman who hasn't been cowed by you. You wouldn't know when to stop.*

Peyton would keep me in line.

So you'd force the woman to do what you should— exercise a little self discipline. You're a fine specimen, Cass Sloane! Do the honorable thing and see her home without indulging in your own warped fantasies.

Peyton pierced the last bite of cream puff with her fork and brought it to her lips. She chewed it slowly, savoring the sweet creaminess while Cass watched. And watched.

He didn't seem to be able to tear his eyes from her, and again Peyton sensed that eerie connection with him. As if he needed something she had to give. As if her heightened awareness of him went both ways.

They sat in silence, though they were surrounded by the sounds of clinking glasses and silverware on plates. The band played on, but Peyton and Cass simply watched each other, wondering, mute.

"It's getting late," Peyton said finally. "We should be going."

Cass studied the check and tucked a few dollars under a plate for the tip. He paid the bill, and they walked out into the crisp autumn night.

"Why don't I walk you home?" Cass said, finding his voice at last. "After a dinner like that, I could use the exercise."

"All right." Her voice was quiet, almost tentative, as if she'd detected his inner turmoil. Or found some of her own.

They set off. The night was cool, and a quarter moon supplied only modest light, but Peyton seemed to warm the space around them with her own light. When she caught her heel in a crack in the brick street, Cass caught her by the shoulder. The touch sent shock waves coursing to his bones. "Are you okay?" he asked.

She nodded, not trusting her voice. His touch had electrified her. Tonight had proven most unsettling; she hadn't simply imagined the attraction between them. It was as real as the late-season cricket chirping in the alley.

No man had ever looked at her with that raw mixture of agony and ardor she'd seen in Cass tonight. And no man would, unless he were asking for something only a woman—only she—could give.

It frightened her.

But it strengthened and sweetened her attraction for him. And made it that much more dangerous. She simply could not give in. She stood to lose too much. Involvement with her boss threatened her pride, her objectivity, and most of all, her self-respect.

She hadn't achieved what she had by engaging in affairs with men in power. This was no time to start. He wasn't even her type. Too brooding. Too tough. Too cynical.

But his touch had seared her, set every muscle trembling, and she still hadn't recovered. Worse, she didn't *want* to recover.

They'd already arrived at her house before Peyton mustered the courage to ask him. "Why did you do it?" she whispered, half fearing his reply.

"Do what?"

"Touch me. Like this." She lifted her finger to his cheek and traversed the line of his jaw, stopping at the subtle cleft in his chin. His skin was rough from the day's beard. A shiver, whether from nerves or the evening air, tripped down her back.

Cass exhaled carefully. His warm breath enveloped

Peyton's finger. She let it rest on his chin and looked up helplessly. She couldn't explain why she'd reached out to Cass. It could only bring trouble.

"I don't know," he said hoarsely. "You seemed so innocent and fresh. I wanted to capture that and hold onto it. There's so little of that anymore." Cass took her finger from his chin and, covering her hand with his, guided it to rest along the angular plane of his cheek. He gazed down into her eyes, then slowly, with tantalizing caution, he brushed back her hair and encircled her face with his hands.

"This isn't wise," Peyton murmured, but she was too engulfed by the sensation of Cass's skin against hers to move away. Warmth kindled deep within her, penetrated her bones, radiated from her skin. She felt vigorous and alive, her blood racing, breath coming short and shallow.

If she continued to let him hold her, she would regret it. She would never be able to look at him again without remembering this: Cass in the moonlight, caressing her face and hair, a look of utter need written across his features. She should pull away, now, before they compromised objectivity with passion. Before he kissed her.

"You're right," Cass muttered. "This isn't smart." But instead of dropping his hands, he pulled her to him. He wove her hair through his fingers and cupped the back of her head, like a cradle, holding her, supporting her.

His eyes took on a different hue, the blue of an icy stream on the first day of spring, melting ever so slowly around the edges. This close, Peyton wondered how he'd ever seemed remote, removed, emotionless. This close, she suspected he was none of those things.

Acting on instinct, Peyton wound her left arm up his

back and rested it on his well-defined shoulderblade. And waited.

When it came, his kiss was nothing short of electric—a quick, galvanizing jolt followed by a series of longer, equally furious shocks. Cass played it out like a scene in slow motion, lowering his lips little by little to meet Peyton's, as if reluctant to overwhelm her.

He did anyway. He stole her breath away, deliberately, slowly. First he kissed her hard, full-throttle, square on her mouth. Then more leisurely, he took possession of her upper lip, then her lower. He nibbled and teased their suppleness before reclaiming her whole mouth for his own.

Peyton caught one ragged gasp of air before abandoning herself to the stinging power of Cass's kisses. Her heart pounded; the blood surged beneath her skin. He kissed her again, and she was filled with new heat, new energy. She gathered handfuls of thick blond hair to anchor herself to him and began her own assault. She explored the contours of Cass's lips and mouth, melding herself to him, eager as she had not been eager before. She rained caresses down his throat, tucking her head in the hollow at his throat.

Cass countered by sprinkling her ear with short, hot puffs of breath, needy, wanting, urging her to take what she desired, what he desired as well.

Peyton thought she could stay in his arms forever.

Cass sealed his lips to Peyton's before demanding entrance to her mouth. He tasted of spice, cool, sweet custard, and malt and barley, rich and fermented. He probed her mouth skillfully. Peyton welcomed each stroke, answering with equal strength.

What was she doing? This was madness!

And if it were, she didn't want it to end. She pushed aside caution and let excitement blaze up and consume it. She pulled Cass closer, fanning the flames of desire. She felt his length against her, tall and muscular, a presence she could learn to rely on.

Cass groaned deep in his throat. "Peyton. Oh, Peyton."

Then, as if summoning the last remnants of strength, he pushed her away, gently, lacking the force to do anything harsh, softening the blow of rejection. But it was rejection nonetheless.

She stood there in the moonlight, inhaling the crisp night air in raspy jags. Still shaking from the power of his kiss and its unexpected end, she stepped back. She released her grip on Cass's body abruptly, as if she'd been holding a live wire and only now recognized the danger it posed. That Cass posed. She stared at his bruised and swollen lips, wondering idly if hers matched his, knowing that they did.

The understanding between them would never be the same. How could it, with this much passion between them? And how could they get past tonight to tomorrow?

"This is not a good idea," she whispered. "Not a good idea at all." *Not even if I want it,* she thought. *Not even if this man makes me feel more alive than anyone I've ever met.*

"You're right. And not for the first time today. I should learn to trust your judgment." He took two steps back, a deep breath. "It won't happen again."

He turned, strode down the front walk, and disappeared down the brick street into the darkness.

THREE

Cass proved as good as his word. There were no more kisses in the moonlight, no stray caresses across Peyton's cheek. He was cordial but distant, never edging beyond the bounds of professional courtesy.

That distance allowed Peyton to recoup her perspective and rebuild their working relationship. She kept busy implementing the changes he had outlined for the station. "On Air Columbus" became an overnight sensation, and Peyton's other ideas did her credit, too. She developed a model training program for her college interns; three other stations asked for her help to copy it. She worked on new angles for "Top Kid"—taking the program on location to schools and community centers and exploring the idea of using youngsters for some of the talent.

But in the quiet moments, at her desk or in her bed, she'd relive those hours over dinner. Cass had touched her heart with his need. In turn, she'd responded to his icy hot touch with a ferocity that she hadn't known she possessed. His kisses had struck chords that still resonated.

A month later, Peyton still hadn't discovered how to silence them.

She treasured the incandescent memory of her own desire, the connectedness she'd felt with Cass. But she didn't see that anguished hunger in Cass's eyes again; he kept himself under tight control.

And she followed suit, unwilling to risk her professionalism again. Not for one weak moment, however delicious.

Cass wasn't interested in romance. He didn't have a heart any more, not one worth sharing. He told himself that half a dozen times a day. Yet that same half a dozen times a day he would roam the station floor, unconsciously watching for Peyton, listening for her clear, mellow voice. And on one such foray, she cornered him outside her office.

"Cass, I've got a deal you can't refuse." She smiled brightly. "I want to put you on the lecture circuit."

"Hmm?"

"You know I teach radio production at Ohio State."

Cass nodded. Contrary to his normal practices, he'd made a point of finding out all he could about Peyton. And the woman amazed him—the station ran smoothly despite her added duties as his producer, her second career as a teacher, and her chairmanship of the annual radio executives' association meeting.

She was bright, ambitious, and competent. The more he learned about her, the more he was attracted to her and the more he struggled to keep that attraction buried. Wasn't this just like Fate—to throw Peyton in his path when he wasn't capable of more than wanting her? She deserved so much better than that.

"The class gets really dull when I do nothing but lecture," she continued. "So I bring in a lot of guest speakers. And I have the perfect opening for you! Next Tuesday at 9:00. Your topic is the future of AM radio.''

"Now wait a minute!" Cass protested. He didn't want more after-hours encounters with Peyton. He'd promised himself. "I have a radio show to do five nights a week."

"I have it all planned," Peyton shot back. "In this technologically amazing age, you *can* be in two places at once. You do the first segment of the show live, then leave the engineer with tapes for the second. My class runs until 10:00, so you'll have plenty of time for your talk and to take questions. We meet in Arps Hall, room 212. I'll get you a parking pass."

"Whoa, Peyton! I don't remember saying yes."

"There's nothing to it. I'll even supply the questions I want you to address in your talk."

"Always the producer, aren't you?"

"Just anticipating objections." Peyton opened the door to her office with a subtle nudge of her hip, then cocked her head at him. Her eyes twinkled mischievously. "I'll pay you. Bremen Brat platters at Rainer's. *My* treat."

"Bribery's not necessary," he countered, but her offer caught him off guard. Was she flirting with him? Asking for a repeat performance of their last meal there? What sort of social conventions ruled these days anyway?

"Give me the questions by Friday, and I'll talk to your class." It was easier than giving in to dinner. But not nearly so pleasant.

"Thanks! I owe you." She crossed the threshold into her office and motioned for Cass to follow her. She riffled through a pile of papers on her desk, pulled out three typed sheets and handed them to Cass.

He looked at them and lifted his eyebrows. "My questions already? You were pretty sure of yourself."

"On tape if nothing else. But in person is so much more effective. Thanks."

The cheerful smile she shot his way made Cass ache for another. He should leave, but he couldn't seem to tear himself away. He stood in the doorway, alternately studying the questions and Peyton, hoping for . . . a few more minutes together.

Peyton's scalp tingled as she realized Cass was still there. He leaned quietly against the door jamb, watching her organize ad scripts. A shiver of awareness scurried down her spine, and she stiffened involuntarily. What was he doing, after so many weeks of carefully avoiding her?

If he wanted to rattle her, make her nervous, he was succeeding. Peyton waited a minute, then two, and finally looked up directly at him. In that moment she caught sight of that same fierce hunger she'd seen four weeks ago. It radiated through his eyes and across his face. It flickered as Cass realized Peyton was watching him, then blinked out completely.

"I think I can handle these questions," he said abruptly and backed out of the door. "Next Tuesday, right?"

"Yes." Peyton almost strangled on the word. "Let me know if I can clarify anything."

He had done nothing—not a word, not a touch. Yet her heart was marking triple time, and her palms were moist. And it was all because she thought she read something in his eyes. Those wonderful blue eyes!

Something about him was calling to her. She couldn't be mistaken about that. But what did it mean?

Nothing's gone right today, Cass fumed to himself. It started out badly, with a flat tire on his Jeep. The day had deteriorated from there.

The meeting with the account execs hadn't yielded the expected results, and a session with the FM program director had convinced him that that band's market share was a total fluke.

And it was October 11. Eighteen years ago today, he and Katie had taken their wedding vows in the little Methodist church around the corner from her parents' house. It had been such a wonderful beginning, one of those clear Ohio October days, with the leaves beginning to turn their brilliant shades of scarlet and gold.

It would still be wonderful if he'd had the sense God gave a goat and done what Katie had asked him—begged him—to do. Come home. It had been her turn. She'd followed him around the country for years as he made a name—and a fortune—for himself. He still had part of the fortune, but nothing else. His marriage was gone—shattered in a single night. All he had left now was guilt.

If they'd come home, she'd still be alive. If they'd come home, they'd have a family, little golden daughters who'd have their dad wrapped around their fingers. And a son to toss a baseball with, to show how to plant a garden.

Cass smashed his fist against the heavy glass desk, nearly shattering it with the force of his blow. This was too painful, playing "what might have been." It didn't do him or the station any good. He had to save his memories for the quiet of the night, when he was alone. So alone.

He flexed his throbbing fist. Nothing broken, it seemed. He stood and walked to the door. He'd go down to the studio to check on preparations for tonight's broadcast. Maybe he could get control of himself in the announcer's chair.

It was Peter, Peyton's quirkiest intern, who broke the bad news about "On Air Columbus."

"I just took the calls, Mr. S." Peter said, blinking rapidly behind his wire rim glasses. "Senator Glenn has to be on the Senate floor tonight for an important roll call vote. And the Bengals' secretary called, too. The quarterback's traveling with the general manager, and their plane is late. They'll still be in the air at eight, with no air phone. I think that means we're out of guests."

"Damn and double damn. Where's Peyton?" Cass demanded.

"I don't know. We're trying to find her. I think we have back-up tapes, but I don't know where."

"Why not? Isn't that one of your jobs around here? What good is an intern who doesn't know where the tapes for his show are?" As Peter stood there dumbly, Cass barked, "Well? Start looking!"

"Yes, sir!" Peter took one step back, then another before turning to flee the control booth.

Cass muttered oaths as he searched the cabinets. Where was his blasted producer? Where were the blasted tapes? If either or both didn't materialize soon, he'd be forced to use open phones for the evening's show. He hated only one thing more than this kind of screw-up. Open phone lines with no topic. There was no controlling those callers, and Cass demanded control in every situation. There would be, he promised himself, hell to pay for this one.

Peyton breezed in at a quarter to six.

"Where have you been?" Cass snapped. "We've been looking all over for you."

"I had to run some errands."

"*Errands?* Before a broadcast? What were you thinking of?"

"I was thinking I had to deposit the station's receipts because Phil didn't have time to do it today. What's the matter?"

"Both Senator Glenn and the Bengals called. They've cancelled. No one knows where you've hidden the back-up tapes, and I for one hate this kind of foul up. How's that for openers?"

"Tough afternoon," she said mildly. "But we've got over an hour to fix things up. Don't worry."

"Don't worry? My reputation's on the line, and you're telling me not to worry?"

"That's exactly what I'm telling you. We've got that terrific interview with the football coach at Ohio State. There's a home game this Saturday, so it's appropriate. He may even be willing to give us half an hour tonight for questions. As for the second half . . ." Peyton paused, thinking. She chewed her lower lip and closed her eyes while Cass paced, irritated.

"I've got it!" she said. "It's fall, right? Back to school time. Let's start a new series on education opportunities here in Franklin County."

"Nothing like a spur of the moment series," Cass spat sarcastically.

Peyton rushed on, undaunted. "We can start with Ohio State's extension program. I teach there, so you can talk to me for a while. I have a course catalog at the station; I can bluff my way through the basic questions.

"And if I'm not enough to suit you," she added, "I have the Dean's number. He'll be glad for some free publicity. And tomorrow we'll call the folks at the Community Education Center, Otterbein, Capital. . . . It's perfect."

"What else do we have on tape?" Cass asked.

"Reruns," she said, certain Cass would reject the

idea. Reruns, he was fond of saying, defeated the whole purpose of radio. You had to stay fresh, innovative and new every day of the year.

"Absolutely not. What else?"

"Mostly fluff: the county home economist on putting up apple butter, the mayor giving Trick or Treat tips, that sort of thing. Trust me, we don't want to use all our tapes at once. The back to school idea is great stuff. We can even tie it in with the football interview—you know, school and fun go hand in hand."

"I don't like it. The balance is wrong; there's nothing hard-hitting."

"Would you rather have dead air? Open phones?" Cass growled.

"We don't have much time," Peyton pointed out. "If you don't like this idea, you'd better come up with another. I only have an hour to arrange for guests."

Cass paced the small studio as Peyton located the coach's interview tape. What was Cass's problem? He'd worked in radio long enough to know that guests often cancelled. More than once she'd had to make do with what she had. And everything would be fine. More or less. But Cass was acting as if it were *her* fault, and that didn't sit well with her. She'd accept responsibility for problems she might cause, but she refused to shoulder the blame for a situation beyond her control, something which she would rectify as best she could.

"Where was that tape?" Cass stormed.

"In the cassette bin marked 'On Air Columbus,' " Peyton said with exaggerated patience. "Now, do I call Dean Woolverton or not?"

"Not much choice. But this is never to happen again. I want to know exactly where the tapes are filed, and I want the interns to know exactly where the tapes are filed. And I want more back-ups. This quantity—and quality—is pathetic! What were you thinking of when you booked them?"

"*You* approved every one of those ideas," she said quietly. "If you don't like them, blame yourself." She lifted her chin and gazed steadily into Cass's eyes. "I'm leaving now to make the calls that'll get this education series on the air," she continued. "I hope you're feeling a bit more human when airtime rolls around." She turned on her heel and walked out, shaking.

How dare he? He was behaving like a lunatic, exactly as she might have expected him to act before she'd come to respect his talent and judgment. But now, after weeks of a decent working relationship and the hint of something deeper . . . why, he'd turned into Mr. Hyde! And after that tantrum, she thought angrily, he deserved to float in his own soup. He'd come out slugging, assigning blame and berating everyone within earshot.

She glanced at her watch. Forty-five minutes to air. She might as well make herself look good—and keep up the public's opinion of the show.

She picked up the phone and dialed. "Hello, Dean Woolverton. It's Peyton Adair . . ."

The show was a remarkable success. The listeners loved the idea of back to school for adults. Calls poured in from all over town, and Peyton was pleased. The interns were amazed at the way she'd pulled things together.

Only Cass didn't seem happy. At the end of the broadcast, he jerked off his headphones and stalked out without so much as a word of thanks.

"Good night, Peyton, and thanks for saving the show," she shouted as Cass slammed the door to the studio.

Cass's behavior wasn't fair, and she wasn't going to accept it. If he hadn't apologized by tomorrow evening—good grief! Cass was supposed to speak to her class tomorrow! In his current state of mind, whatever had triggered it, she wouldn't put it past him to cancel on *her* exactly as his guests had tonight!

She shrugged. So be it. Changes were part of the business of radio. Her class might as well learn to be flexible now; they'd need that skill in their careers.

Sighing, she put away the last of the tapes and turned out the lights.

In the parking lot, Cass threw his Jeep into gear and roared down the street. He was furious—more at himself than at Peyton. He'd allowed his own problems and memories to cloud his judgment, and he'd hammered at Peyton's professionalism and dedication without a second thought. He unzipped the side window and breathed deeply. The cold night air burned his lungs.

He'd done it again—just like his first day on the job. He'd gone into the attack mode when no one was at fault—exactly the behavior he'd come home to rid himself of. But in the heat of the moment, his killer instinct broke loose—the one that had built number one stations while earning him the reputation of a tyrannical perfectionist.

When he'd left New York, no one had understood what he was trying to accomplish. He was popular with the listeners, and he was wildly successful behind the scenes. What more could he want? Certainly not a village in central Ohio whose main claim to fame was a Fourth of July festival and fish fry!

But Cass had been determined. He *would* recapture something of the man he'd once been. He'd spent the first few weeks in Ohio trying to shed his hardboiled New York persona. He rebuilt the old clapboard house that had been Katie's legacy to him, sweating despite the March winds as he nailed shingles and shutters in place and scraped and repainted the siding. Instinctively, he knew not to hire a band of Columbus renovators; slowly his neighbors came around to offer a hand and talk a bit. No one here seemed to find it strange that he'd returned; *their* only surprise was that he and Katie had ever left.

He kept a conscious check on the arrogance he had encouraged in New York, and slowly he wove himself into the warp and woof of Ashville "society."

The opportunity at WFKN had been an unexpected boon. Cass hadn't thought about work when he left the city; he had more than enough money to survive for a long time in Ashville. Now he wondered if he hadn't made a big mistake. Would he ever find a way to rein in his instinct for the jugular and reclaim his soul, what Katie had loved, and still run a million dollar radio station?

In the meantime, he owed Peyton an apology.

Peyton. She was the truly unexpected gift he'd found when he'd come back. The one he wasn't ready for.

Unbidden, the scent and weight of Peyton's auburn hair claimed him. He recalled the touch of it, threading its way through his fingers. A man could lose himself in it. And her lips, pliant and yet ardent. The memory of their kisses burned, and an unfamiliar sensation of warmth spread through his limbs.

Want, he told his body sternly, *is not a factor here. Regrets are. Never mind that apologies have never been my strong suit. I have to make her understand that tonight was an aberration, that I can control myself better than I did.*

I don't want to lose her. Not as a program director, not as a producer. Not as a woman.

Cass didn't go to the station the next evening until

after six. He found a neatly detailed list of guests, telephone numbers and questions for the evening's broadcast, but there was no sign of Peyton.

She was angry—and with good reason. Perhaps she was trying to show him how difficult work would be without her, or perhaps . . . No, she surely wouldn't think he'd be so unprofessional as not to show up when he'd promised.

On the other hand, he'd behaved most unprofessionally last night. Maybe she'd be justified in thinking he'd behave just as badly tonight.

He'd simply have to prove her wrong.

Cass slipped into her classroom at five minutes to nine. His appearance clearly startled her. She lost her place in her notes and grew flustered before she recovered enough to finish her comments on daily operations.

"Mr. Sloane, I'm glad you're feeling better. I wasn't sure you were going to make it." No trace of warmth marked her tone, and her gray eyes were hard as flint. She made his introduction sparse, strictly business.

Her class, however, was delighted that Cass had come. They greeted him with applause as he stood to take Peyton's place at the podium.

"Thank you," Cass began. "As I'm sure Ms. Adair has told you, the radio business is always hectic, and sometimes it feels like you're working in hell. In the radio business, you're filling the airwaves with music, talk or news twenty-four hours a day. Think of it. There's not a moment's rest for the equipment—or the management.

"Sometimes things go wrong. Seriously wrong. Your satellite link dissolves or your transmitter blows, and you're off the air—or a guest cancels at the last minute, leaving you with an hour of airtime to fill."

What is the point of this? Peyton thought, irritated.

*He's not going to rehash last night and chastise me
again, is he? Because I don't deserve it, and I won't
allow it—not in my class!*

"Case in point," Cass said. "Yesterday both Senator
Glenn and the quarterback of the Bengals were scheduled on 'On Air Columbus.' Both cancelled at five-
thirty, and we air at seven."

"Mr. Sloane," Peyton interposed coldly, "I don't
think the class needs to hear about this sort of alterca-
tion. I wanted you to address the question of buyouts
and the future of AM radio."

"I'm getting to that, Ms. Adair," Cass said
smoothly. "Anyway, last night I was irate, as only a
host whose show has just gone down the tubes can be.
I blamed everyone and everything except the fact that
radio *is* that way sometimes. But Ms. Adair, my producer and program director, stayed calm and unflappable. In less than an hour she put together a program
that worked, one that we're going to continue all this
week."

Calm? Unflappable? Peyton couldn't believe what
she was hearing. She'd been livid, hurt—she'd only
saved the show because she was so angry, and her
nature insisted she find positive ways to deal with that
emotion. And maybe just a little so that Cass would
have no justification for his accusations. But calm and
unflappable?

"You need to know that about radio. Sometimes
your boss can be brutally unfair, and you have to tough
it out because listeners are depending on your station
to keep them in touch with the world."

Unfair. Her boss had been unfair, and he was admit-
ting it! Peyton was shocked. It wasn't quite an apology;
heck, he hadn't even apologized for the greater impro-

priety of rousing feelings she hadn't known she had. But it might be as good as she got.

Cass talked on, animated, about the steps taken in WFKN's buyout and the subsequent changes in format. Students interrupted from time to time with questions, and the last hour of the class turned lively.

"You were a hit." She kept her voice neutral as she gathered her notes from her lectern.

"Except with you."

"Oh?" She kept her eyes on her stack of notes. She didn't dare face him. The pain was still too close to the surface, and she didn't care to expose herself to another firestorm.

"You're still annoyed with me about yesterday."

"Is that what you think?"

"Yes. You didn't give me much of an introduction. And the note you left in the studio won't win any awards for warmth." Cass plunged his hands into the pockets of his black tweed jacket. "You're angry."

Peyton took a deep breath and counted to ten. If he wanted a rise out of her, he'd chosen the right night. She wasn't prepared to take any more flak from Cass Sloane. Hemi-semi-demi apology or not, he'd as good as asked for her opinion. And was he going to get it.

"I have a right to be. I did a damn good job saving yesterday's broadcast, and I'll bet tonight's show was even better. But I don't even get a thank you. Instead, I'm belittled and scolded as if I were anything but a professional." She stuffed her notes into a leather portfolio and snapped it shut. "Well, I think that's a lousy way to run a radio station. And I deserve a real apology."

"I thought I'd given you one. Right now, in front of your whole class. I called myself unfair."

"Recognizing what you are isn't the same thing as

saying you're sorry." Peyton spoke in clipped syllables as she pulled on a short blue wool jacket and shouldered her purse. "It's late. Good night, Mr. Sloane."

"We're back to Mr. Sloane?"

"I prefer not to use first names with people who can't show me any respect." She picked up her briefcase and began to walk towards the door.

"Peyton!" Cass's tone was commanding and dark.

"Yes?" She turned around, her face schooled in stone. Only her short, shallow breathing gave any indication what she felt.

Cass reached out and put a hand on either of Peyton's shoulders. Keeping her at arm's length, he said, "It has been an extremely trying couple of days. Try to understand that."

"That's no excuse for your behavior." Peyton was implacable. "You don't let your personal trials interfere with business. Likewise you don't mix personal pleasures with business." She lifted her chin and gazed straight into his eyes. He would not mistake how serious she was about this.

And then she saw it again, the look that haunted Cass—the hurt, the ache, the trapped silence. It broke through for a fleeting instant, then winked out.

Peyton tilted her head down, staring at Cass's red tie. The paisley pattern hurt her eyes, but she couldn't bring herself to look directly at him again. She would surely melt and forgive him. And to offer forgiveness when he hadn't asked for it could only encourage his special breed of arrogance.

Cass's hands tightened around her shoulders, and Peyton could feel the warmth of his body through three layers of clothing. She was weakening. She truly hated beings at odds with people. Her insides were turning to mush, and soon she'd be crying for him to forgive *her* for any real or imaginary offenses.

"I'm sorry." His voice was barely a whisper. Peyton had to strain to hear him. Then in a stronger tone Cass continued, "It *has* been a difficult time for me, but I shouldn't have gone haywire on you. I know you wouldn't let the station or our listeners down."

"Or you, either." Peyton broke her stare from the paisley tie and looked up at Cass with genuine concern. She read uncertainty and confusion in his face, and her small store of fortitude collapsed. She wanted to take his face between her hands and kiss away the sorrow, offer him the safe harbor of her heart. But she couldn't do that, not with Cass. It was too risky, too fraught with problems, real and potential.

She tried the banter they'd established as their stock-in-trade conversation. "I was so surprised by yesterday. I thought I'd come to know a general manager who wasn't anything like all the stories I'd heard. Then, kapow! They all came true."

"Forgive me?"

Peyton smiled tentatively. "Sure." She had to get out into the night air. It was too hot in here to think clearly. She'd almost reached up and kissed him!

"Prove it," Cass said quietly. In an instant the yard between them was bridged, and Peyton was home in his arms again. He smothered her with his mouth, and his hands reached down to her waist and behind her jacket. He explored her back through the softness of her angora sweater, pressing and kneading the heated flesh with the expertise of a knowing lover.

Peyton's insides ran together like candle wax surrounded by flame. Cass was back, touching her and building the passion inside her.

Her memory had exaggerated nothing about him.

Cass was powerful, tender, and uniquely able to tap unplumbed rivers of sensation deep within her. The glow of exhilaration threaded through her and made her weak with need.

Peyton dropped her briefcase to the floor, freeing her hands for more pleasurable tasks. She braced herself, palms down on his chest, and moved her hands in lazy circles. She marveled at the feel of him beneath the tight weave of his cotton shirt. She rubbed her thumb slowly and deliberately across his nipple, hardening it like the rest of his body. Then she snaked her arms around his side and traced idle, random patterns on his back with her nails.

Cass kissed her hair, her eyes, her neck. Impatient, he slipped the jacket off her shoulders and sent it to join the briefcase on the floor. Only the soft green wool of her sweater separated his hands from her skin. In seconds he had scooped up the fabric to let his fingers rest on the precious prize of her flesh.

He played brilliant melodies on her back, each finger drawing forth point and counterpoint. Peyton felt her bones melt into the music, and she hung on to Cass with what strength she still had.

A little voice tried to shout above the wild sensations dancing on her skin that this was insane, that Cass was not the man for her. He had too many secrets, and he was too reticent about sharing his real self. But Peyton ignored caution. She felt too right holding him as close as he held her, kissing away the demons of insecurity and perfectionism that tormented him.

She was a goner. She knew that as certainly as she knew her own name. She pulled Cass even closer, showering him with rapid kisses across his mouth and face. Then boldly, she pressed her lips to his and wedged her tongue between his teeth. She felt the sharp edges of his incisors, then knew pure delight as he opened his mouth to admit her. His tongue curled around hers in welcome. Their kisses grew so deep and intimate that Peyton nearly collapsed from the heady pleasure. But she found in Cass a rock of support.

Her hands roamed his torso, memorizing every inch of his perfect body. She felt the strain in his lower limbs, and she moved her stomach suggestively across his manhood.

"Oh, Cass," she murmured, coming up for air. She leaned back in the circle of Cass's arms to study his flushed features. He was wonderfully handsome, strikingly male. And he made her feel so alive, so richly female. There could be nothing wrong with that.

They would build a bridge of trust. They had to. Peyton never wanted to leave the safety of his arms, never wanted to return to earth without Cass beside her.

"Peyton," Cass responded hoarsely, stroking her hair with one hand and cupping one perfect buttock with the other. "This is all wrong, and I can't help myself. I promised you this would never happen again. This is another apology I owe you."

"Shh. No offense given or taken. I want you, too. Can't you see that?"

I want you, too. The words echoed in her ears, in her heart. They were truer than she'd imagined, even five minutes ago. Where did this all fit in? The passion, the confusion, reconciling dreams and hearts, old behavior and new? Peyton had never tried this before— meshing her public and private lives; she'd been convinced it only led to trouble. She'd just chastised Cass for doing exactly that.

And yet, now that she'd found Cass and admitted the truth, she could have it no other way.

"I'm sorry," he muttered. He pulled his hands away,

broke the embrace. As much as he wanted Peyton, as deep as his need for her ran, he had to stop. This was getting perilously close to intimacy and involvement.

And he had no room in his life for either of those attachments. He'd embraced them once, and they'd nearly destroyed him when he lost Katie. He would never allow himself to experience either again.

Peyton had proved that he still had primitive passions: desire and want. With another woman he might have given in to those passions—given and taken pleasure and release. But Peyton deserved better. She deserved love, the love of a man who hadn't been hopelessly scarred by heartache.

As he had been. He could never be what she needed. He could offer her nothing but sadness and secrets too bitter to share.

His face clouded with the same restless shadow Peyton had seen before. "What's the matter?" she whispered, frightened. "You're hurt. Let me help you!"

"It's an old pain, Peyton. There's no help for it." He reached down to pick up her jacket and tenderly draped it around her shoulders. "I'm not going to start something I can't finish. Besides, I have to get back to the studio."

"Don't do this to me!" she cried, desperate. "I'm going crazy for you and you're putting an end to this?"

"Yes." He made his voice steely, though it cost him every ounce of strength he had left. "Now let's get out of here before I do something we'll both regret."

"Don't flatter yourself. You wouldn't do anything I didn't want you to do." Then her tone softened and she pleaded, "Can't we just try? There's something magic between us. I felt it the day we met. If we don't give it a chance, *that's* what we'll both regret."

He couldn't. If he let Peyton in now, he would be

opening himself to the very possibilities he'd closed off five years ago.

He stepped back, away from Peyton's warmth. But he couldn't escape her upturned face, still radiating hope. "This is a mistake," he said. "A terrible mistake."

His subconscious prodded him. *This is why you came home. To reclaim the kind of man you were. To find peace.*

But not like this!

His gaze met hers, and agitation shot through his eyes. Something was holding him back, Peyton realized. Something was keeping him from acknowledging in words the tremendous pull between them.

"Don't be afraid," she whispered. "It'll be all right."

"It's a mistake," he repeated.

But when Peyton opened her arms and gathered him in, his resistance lacked conviction.

"How could it be a mistake?" she asked softly, resting her head under his chin.

Cass had no answer that made sense.

FOUR

"Cass!" Peyton barely paused to knock at his office door before poking her head in to see if he was in. "Look at this!"

She waved a letter high over her head like a New Year's Eve noisemaker.

Cass turned from the computer screen and an uncooperative spreadsheet program. "What is it?" Cass asked, smiling at Peyton's obvious delight.

"It's an invitation to be a judge at the Little Miss Pumpkin Show contest in Circleville! Listen: 'Dear Ms. Adair: In recognition of your contribution to children's programming in the central Ohio area, the board of Pumpkin Show, Inc., the Greatest Free Show on Earth, invites you to serve as a judge for the Little Miss Pumpkin Show contest, on Wednesday, October 18.''

"Now, isn't that a coup?" Cass teased.

"It's proof that 'Top Kid' is still reaching its audience—despite the time changes. Adults are taking notice, too."

"Are you going to accept?"

56

"I've already called them. I'd never turn down free publicity for the station. In fact, I think we should adopt the Pumpkin Show and try to encourage our listeners to attend. The week before, we can tease our listeners and tell them we'll be there, where we'll be, how to stop by for prizes. Then we should take the mobile unit to Circleville for opening day and do a few live remote broadcasts to get people excited about the festival. I could do a short interview with the Little Miss, too, for 'Top Kid.' "

"Have you ever been to the Pumpkin Show?" Cass asked, shaking his head at her unbridled enthusiasm.

"No, but every fall I read about it. The pumpkin tower, pumpkin waffles, pumpkin doughnuts, pumpkin ice cream, pumpkin fudge, the six foot pumpkin pie . . . I've been wanting to go for years. This is a great opportunity!"

"Better than the Michigan State Fair," Cass observed dryly.

"Where's your sense of place?" Peyton chided him. "This is a small town festival celebrating autumn and the harvest; it's everything that's near and dear to our listeners. You'd better leave that sophisticated New York facade behind if you're coming with me!"

"When did I say I was coming with you?"

Peyton's eyes twinkled wickedly. "Somebody's got to come. I can't judge the contest and give away prizes and do live remotes all at the same time. I thought you might be agreeable." She leaned over and said in a stage whisper, "You could give this poor deprived Michigander a lesson in Ohio history."

Cass spread his hands in surrender. "I give up. Let's mark the calendar now. And let's be sure we've got plenty of stories in the can for 'On Air Columbus' that evening. Who knows, maybe we'll want to ride the Ferris wheel all night!''

Peyton grinned and breezed out of Cass's office, pleased as punch that she'd been able to convince Cass to join her. Since her startling admission that she was "crazy for him," she'd racked her brains for clues to what made him alternately so passionate and so withdrawn.

It surprised her to realize that she could feel so strongly about someone she knew so little about, but her feelings were undeniable. She positively glowed when she thought of him. Her stomach flipflopped when she saw him, and her step took on added spring when she walked beside him. There was admiration in her eyes when they talked about the station. And when she kissed him . . .

Ahhh . . . his kisses could curl her toes.

But what did she really know of him except his professional background? Nothing about his childhood, his youth, his schooling. He'd been married, but even about that she knew precious little. But it seemed that friendship had caught fire, pairing them in a most unlikely combination.

But for some reason, Cass was reluctant to act on their obvious attraction. So it pleased Peyton that she'd have a whole day with him outside the office. They'd go to the Pumpkin Show, ostensibly for business, but also so she could get to know the man who'd laid vigorous claim to her emotions.

She knew what attracted her, of course. Physically, he was gorgeous. His height, his erect carriage, and his powerful build all contributed to his commanding presence. He radiated power and self-assurance, and Peyton felt charged by that energy. His knowledge was built on years of experience, and she felt a mentoring closeness she hadn't experienced since her teen years.

But most important, he needed her. She'd seen it in his eyes the first time he'd kissed her and again the second time—a deep unquenchable thirst for her. She would have thought the cosmopolitan Cass would have wanted someone more worldly-wise, more in tune with sophistication. But he'd chosen her.

The thought made her giddy. What had he said? She was innocent and fresh. She still had the wide-eyed enthusiasm that some people never lose, that keeps them young past old age.

Suddenly it struck her. Cass had lost or misplaced or buried his zest for life. She saw that clearly: his by-the-numbers programming and his meticulous attention to detail were just symptoms of a man who'd detached his heart from the joy of living.

But he had a heart. It was already bound with hers. She just had to help him reconnect it beyond their relationship, to include the rest of his life. She smiled, clutching the Pumpkin Show invitation to her breast, and hurried down the hall. She had a lot to do before next Wednesday.

The day of the Pumpkin Show dawned bright and clear, the last of the Indian summer days they had any right to expect. It felt deliciously naughty to be skipping work in the middle of the week, even though Peyton would be promoting the station all day.

I'm acting like a kid, she told herself, but that didn't stop her from dancing around her bedroom, trying to decide what a judge would wear to the Pumpkin Show. She finally settled on autumn tones: a pair of brown gabardine pants, a butter colored cotton turtleneck, and a short tweed bomber jacket. On the jacket collar, she carefully pinned the orange "King Pumpkin" that the festival officials had sent with the invitation. Then she pulled her hair up into a thick ponytail and applied her makeup, hiding the faint circles under her eyes that proved she'd been too keyed up to sleep last night.

With a last stroke of the powder brush, she looked at herself critically. She would never be beautiful in the way of models or Miss Americas, but she had a healthy shine about her that was appealing. Her nose turned up the tiniest bit in her oval face, and if she smiled deeply enough, a dimple appeared in her right cheek. She'd lost a couple of pounds since the station takeover, but today should take care of that. She planned to sample every pumpkin delicacy the town had to offer.

She tried to read for the next hour before going to pick Cass up, but she couldn't concentrate. She twirled the dial on her stereo, listening for the competition's new gimmicks and strategies, but that didn't hold her interest, either. She was too eager for the afternoon to begin, with its parade and high school bands and mylar and crepe paper floats.

She arrived at Cass's comfortable frame house half an hour ahead of schedule. When Cass opened the door, he wore a plaid flannel robe. A green bath towel hung around his neck, and his hair stood in damp peaks.

"I'm sorry," she said. "I know I'm early. Take your time getting dressed."

"Come on in." He held the screen door open to let her pass, then led her down a hall to the kitchen. "There's a pot of coffee in here. Cups are in the cupboard nearest the sink."

So this is where Cass lives, Peyton thought. The kitchen was homey, not at all what she would have expected, given the chrome and leather of his office and the tailored suits and ties of his everyday wardrobe.

She would have expected his home to be more of the same.

But it wasn't. The kitchen walls were a pale federal blue with clean white woodwork. A plain white gas range stood across from an old-fashioned porcelain sink. Above the sink, a large window looked out over acres of farmland. In the field she could see a few shocks of corn standing guard over the house.

It's like a Norman Rockwell painting, she thought, hugging the knowledge to herself. It was a far cry from the high tech taskmaster at the station, and it gave her hope.

She reached into the maple cabinet and pulled down a gray stoneware cup and saucer. Thoughtfully she poured herself a cup of coffee and wandered into the dining room. A handsome oblong oak table with twelve matching chairs graced the center of the room. A huge matching hutch gleamed with silver and brass. These were obviously family pieces, and Peyton felt slightly intimidated by the ornate coffee service and chafing dishes sitting on the sideboard. Her family had never owned anything like this.

Cass's study adjoined the dining room. Peyton felt immediately at home as she peered in. A large blue afghan covered a worn sofa, and a leather recliner sat opposite the television. Two double hung windows and a skylight let in plenty of sunlight or moonlight, and the wallpaper looked old and slightly faded.

A small fireplace occupied half of one wall, and from the ashes, Peyton could tell it was still functional. This was obviously where Cass spent most of his time, and she approved. It was comfortable and cozy, a delightful retreat against a cold day or tough decisions.

She wandered over to one of the built-in bookshelves. Cass had an assortment of hardcover textbooks and paperback novels, plus a selection of trade journals to which she also subscribed. But unlike her own book-shelves, he had no assortment of knickknacks decorat-ing the shelves. The only adornment was a solitary silver picture frame.

Peyton picked it up to examine the picture. A photo-graph of a lovely young woman with long blond hair beamed up at Peyton. She sat in a swing under an elm tree, and her face was lit with joy and love.

Stabbed with curiosity, Peyton replaced the photo. It must be Cass's wife. He was not the sort of man who kept a lot of sentimental photographs around; Peyton knew that from the rest of the house.

How had she died? And was she the reason Cass was so reluctant to admit the burning attraction between them?

"Where are you, Peyton?" Cass called, thudding down the stairs from the second floor. "I thought I left you in the kitchen!"

"I'm in here. I went exploring," Peyton said, a little shamefaced. Hadn't her mother always taught her not to take liberties the first time she went visiting?

Cass appeared in the doorway. He wore a long-sleeved blue shirt, beige cords and loafers. He had knotted a navy V-necked sweater around his neck and carried a WFKN windbreaker hooked over his index finger.

Peyton looked at him apologetically. "I'm sorry. I should've stayed put."

"That's okay. There's nothing here to hide."

"This room is wonderful," she confided. "It's so snug and safe."

"I kind of like it, despite the fact that the wallpaper's cracking and the couch needs to be replaced." He looked at Peyton and smiled, and she felt her worry about imposing melt. Only her curiosity remained. "Are you ready to go?"

The fifteen minute drive turned into half an hour because of the festival's opening day traffic. But Cass kept Peyton entertained with tales of Circleville and earlier Pumpkin Shows.

"Circleville, you know, got its name because it was originally built in a circle, behind some prehistoric Indian earthworks. Until the early twentieth century, the courthouse was in the center of town and streets radiated out from it. Then they squared the circle and the whole purpose of the town got lost.

"The Pumpkin Show got started in 1903, when a group of farmers brought their harvest to town and put it on display. Nowadays, there are flower and garden exhibits, home canning displays, an art show, talent contests, and all kinds of free entertainment. There's a little more carny atmosphere than there used to be, what with the midway and rides, but most of the food booths are local. You can snap up some great homemade treats."

"I plan to," Peyton assured him. "How do you know so much about Pumpkin Show? You haven't lived here for years."

"Before my dad retired to Florida, I used to come back to take him to the Pumpkin Show."

It wasn't really a lie. He and Katie *did* take his father down to Circleville. It didn't matter that he wouldn't have come if Katie hadn't always insisted on a fall pilgrimage back home.

"I haven't been back in about five years. I suppose nothing's changed."

"I think it'll be grand." Peyton settled in to absorb the small-town feeling as Cass negotiated the streets to position the van for the three o'clock parade. The President of the Pumpkin Show was waiting to greet them, and Cass proceeded to do a three-minute interview with her. Then, after urging the listeners to come to the festival, Cass and Peyton climbed out of the van to explore the town.

"The celebration doesn't really get started until the chimes are played," the president explained from her perch in a green and orange golf cart. "Climb aboard and let's go watch."

For the next two and a half hours Cass and Peyton roamed the crowded streets, gorging themselves on food and exploring the exhibit halls and craft fair. Peyton had dismissed the president's parting words about being careful of pickpockets; she refused to be concerned about crime in broad daylight. But she noticed Cass seemed especially protective, guiding her by the elbow through the maze of people, paying for their snacks from a wallet he kept tucked in his front pocket.

But aside from that, she had a marvelous time. Cass amazed her with his prodigious memory, rattling off story after story from Ohio history. He seemed open and responsive, answering all her questions about his "misspent youth." He regaled her with tales of sodden Pumpkin Show parades when the weather hadn't cooperated and he'd reeked of his band uniform's wet wool. Peyton didn't know when she'd laughed so hard.

When a little girl named Jennifer was finally selected as queen, Peyton introduced herself to the girl and her parents and asked them to accompany her back to the van for a short interview.

Peyton was heartened to see how easily Cass handled the excited child. He showed her how the equipment worked in the van while Peyton set up for their talk. He presented Jennifer with three WFKN grab bags of prizes when she lisped solemnly, "I mustn't forget my attendants."

Cass acted as engineer for the "Top Kid" segment. When he'd finished, he took the tape and quickly dubbed a second copy.

"Little Miss Pumpkin Show," he said gravely, "this is for you." He handed her the tape. "This is your interview, just the way it'll be on the radio next week."

"Really?" the little girl squealed. "Oh, thank you! I'll never forget this day. Or you either." And she threw her arms around Cass and kissed him soundly on the cheek.

"Jennifer," her mother warned.

"I'm sorry," she said, instantly contrite. "I got too excited."

"That's okay, sweetheart. I like it when pretty girls kiss me."

He's flirting with her! Peyton thought. *I never thought I'd see the day!*

"Thank you, too, Ms. Adair," Jennifer said, tucking her hand inside Peyton's. "I love 'Top Kid.' I listen to it every Sunday. Mom says it's better than cartoons. I can't wait to hear myself on the radio."

Peyton thanked Jennifer and her parents and escorted them out of the van. Then she came back to Cass and said warmly, "You have quite a way with little girls, Mr. Sloane."

"I like little girls," he said. "They're much easier to understand than big ones." He shoved away thoughts of the family he'd never had. "Why don't you go visit that art exhibit? I still have a couple more remotes to do, and there's no sense in both of us being cooped up here."

"Okay," Peyton agreed, glad of the chance to see more of Circleville.

"Just be careful. There are a lot of out-of-towners today, and I don't want you to get hurt."

"Goose," she said, touched at his concern. "I grew up in Detroit. I know how to take care of myself. Besides, it's only dusk, and there are plenty of street lights. What could happen?"

"More than you know, Peyton. More than you know." Cass shook his head and shuddered slightly. Recovering, he pushed her out the van door and said, "Have a good time. Be back by seven o'clock so we can get home at a reasonable hour."

"Will do." She stuffed a leather change purse in the front pocket of her slacks and set off.

Peyton hadn't returned by seven-thirty. By eight o'clock Cass was frantic. Circleville was a small town; you couldn't get lost. A delay of an hour could only mean trouble. Peyton knew the value of time, and he'd seen her wearing a watch today.

Something had happened. He could feel it in his gut. He'd warned her to be careful, and something had still gone wrong. Even though Circleville was a small town, crime paid no attention to population size.

He had to find her. He locked the van and began to search, a hopeless task in the hordes of people that packed the streets waiting for the evening parade. He cruised Court Street, Pinckney, High and Main, growing more desperate with each passing minute. He cursed the parade route that blocked his path on Franklin Street. Finally he decided to check the van once more before reporting the situation to the police.

He found her there, waiting.

"Where have you been?" he thundered. "Do you have any idea how worried I've been?"

Peyton quailed a little before his angry tone. Then

she regained her composure. She was, after all, a grown woman. She could take care of herself.

"I'm sorry I'm late, but you won't believe what happened. I went to the art exhibit and just wandered around. Then I decided I wanted some pumpkin doughnuts—the ones you wouldn't try this afternoon. I finally found the booth, bought them and went off to ride the merry-go-round. There's just something about carousels."

"You're riding the merry-go-round while I'm here sick about you," Cass muttered. "Great, just great."

Peyton ignored him and continued, "Then I went to the craft square again. I saw some great soup bowls I wanted this afternoon. I was ready to come back to the van right after I bought them. But when I went to pay for them, my money was gone."

"I warned you to be careful!" Cass bellowed. "You got your pocket picked, hmm?"

"Cass, shut up and listen," Peyton was tired of his accusatory tone. "I didn't come back right away because I knew you'd react just like this. I thought if I retraced my steps, I might find where I dropped or left it. And if I didn't, then I'd accept the fact that I was pickpocketed."

Cass glowered but said nothing.

"Well, I walked back down the street, stopping at every booth I'd visited and asking about my coin purse. People seemed to remember me, but no one had seen my wallet. Finally I got to the doughnut booth, and the guy there was so happy to see me! He saw me leave it on the counter, but I'd left before he could shout me down. He put it away, hoping I'd come back for it. And I did. This kind of happy ending only happens in small towns, you know."

"I was terrified that you'd been mugged or kidnapped or murdered, and you were busy looking for a coin purse?'' Cass roared. ''A coin purse?''

''It had fifty dollars in it!'' she retorted.

''I suppose you went back and bought the soup bowls, too.''

''No! If it's any consolation, I didn't! I came right back because I knew you'd be worried. But, for goodness sake, Cass, *I'm fine*. I even got my money back. Nothing happened. Why are you so angry?''

''Because you could have gotten yourself killed!''

Peyton felt her previous delight in the day evaporate as they fought. Cass was acting so unreasonable, so out-of-control. The possibility of her getting killed was absurdly remote in small-town Circleville. But something had triggered his rage, and she couldn't believe it was as simple as her being a little late. He frightened her like this; this was worse than any station mishap. This was personal.

She couldn't take him in her arms and soothe his fears; in this mood, he'd only push her away—or worse.

He glared at her until she felt her energy tap out.

''Let's go,'' she said wearily. ''I'm here now, so let's go.'' They climbed into the van.

''Fasten your seat belt,'' Cass barked as he jammed the key into the van's ignition and pulled into traffic. He drove with tightly controlled energy, gripping the wheel until his knuckles fairly glowed with white-edged fury.

What had Peyton been thinking of? he stormed to himself. She was from Detroit, for God's sake. She knew the importance of arriving on time.

Was she out of her mind? Didn't she realize her absence was cause for alarm? Didn't she realize she could have been hurt—or worse?

Worse. The worst. Visions of Katie and that street gang appeared unbidden in his brain: the mind-numbing hours he'd spent until the police had found her, the frozen years he'd spent after he'd buried her.

Now, when he was finally beginning to thaw, it had almost happened again.

No! Gradually he eased his grip on the wheel as the wave of memories receded. It *hadn't* almost happened again. Peyton was all right, damn it! Nothing had happened again. She'd even found her money. Everything was all right.

Except him. He'd just relived the most traumatic event of his life, and not realizing it, had behaved abominably. He'd frightened her; he could see from the stiff way she held herself on the far side of the van.

Peyton deserved more than an apology this time; she deserved an explanation.

_____ FIVE _____

Cass pulled the van into the garage, threw it into park and killed the engine. Peyton could still sense his anger, but somehow it no longer seemed directed at her. She relaxed a fraction, unkinking her shoulders and flexing the fingers she'd kept tightly balled during the ride home.

Now what? An explanation? An apology? An irrefutable reason to call it off? Whatever, it wasn't going to be pleasant.

He opened her door and Peyton slid down the seat to the ground. "Are you warm enough?" he asked, breaking the silence he'd maintained since leaving Circleville. "Can I get you a sweater?"

"I'm fine." She huddled down in her wool jacket.

He picked up an old tarp from a workbench. "Let's walk."

They walked behind Cass's shadowy house into the fields Peyton had seen this morning. An owl screeched once and then twice in the lonely dark. In the fields, Peyton couldn't see the lights of the city; only the full harvest moon and the stars lit their path through corn shocks and wheat stubble.

Whatever troubled him was tearing Cass apart. That much Peyton knew. She wanted to cradle him in her arms and wash away the pain with her kisses. But he had to come to her of his own accord.

That frightened her. He'd been reluctant to act on their attraction all along; perhaps tonight's incident showed why. His behavior had bordered on violence, and she couldn't endure that. If he couldn't share what had disturbed him so greatly . . . She bit her lower lip and blinked rapidly. She wouldn't think of that yet. Not until she had to.

At last they reached a tiny grove of trees. Through their bare branches Peyton could still see the Little Dipper. Cass spread the tarp on the ground and motioned Peyton to sit. A small circle of stones sat neatly on the edge of the grove, and he collected sticks and twigs and laid a campfire.

"You really *were* a Boy Scout," Peyton said, affecting a lightness of tone she didn't feel. Better that than this crushing sense of impending doom.

"Troop 1052," he said as he fanned the fire to life. As the flames licked and cracked the fallen branches, Cass sat beside her and pulled his legs up to his chest.

"I didn't mean to go crazy back there," he started. "You were safe, you had your money, and nothing happened. But I felt absolutely helpless when I didn't know where to find you. It reminded me of another time when I couldn't find someone I loved, and I just went crazy."

Peyton held her breath and let the fire warm her face and fingers.

"My wife, Katie, died five years ago. It was homicide." He paused for a moment, then went on tonelessly. "She was on her way to . . . an appointment. I was meeting her there. I waited and waited, but she never arrived. I went crazy; I didn't know what had happened.

"The police found her body two days later, a block from our home."

"Oh, Cass," Peyton breathed. "I'm so sorry."

"When you didn't come back tonight, I had a horrible panic attack. I didn't recognize what it was until we were driving home. I was reliving those hours when I didn't know where Katie was, when I couldn't find her no matter where I looked. I couldn't stand it."

He hugged his legs closer to his chest, and Peyton slipped her hand over his arm. She didn't want to go too far, but he needed a human touch. This story was too hurtful to bear alone.

"I understand," she said softly. "And I'm sorry. I'm so sorry. I don't ever mean to cause you worry."

"Rage was the only thing I could feel," he said, his voice cracking. "Five years ago, and . . . now. I took it out on you, but it was rage at myself, at the system, at my helplessness."

Peyton looked at him, saw the hurt etched in the rugged creases of his forehead and eyes. Her heart fluttered, missed a beat, then lodged in her throat. She could hardly form her next words. But she had to, even though she dreaded the answer.

"Is that all that's left for you? Rage?"

Cass stared into the fire, poked it with a long stick. The twigs crackled and snapped as a cascade of glowing sparks shot up from the flames. Peyton held her breath, waiting.

"For a long time it was," Cass said finally. "Now . . ." He shrugged. "I'm not sure."

Peyton exhaled quietly, her most important question

answered. A tiny kernel of hope took root in her heart. Gently, gently, she cautioned herself.

"What happened then?"

"I buried her. The police found her killers, two teenage drug addicts. They never went to trial. Instead, the DA offered them a plea bargain they couldn't refuse. It was over in a matter of days."

Cass's jaw twitched, grew tight. His eyes, bone dry, remained fixed on the fire. "I stayed in New York for five more years, working shifts that would've dazed Superman, but I didn't care. I didn't have anything left."

Cass's unshed tears welled up in Peyton, and she blinked sharply to hold them back. What senseless waste, she thought. One tragedy compounded with another. "What happened next?" she prompted softly.

"I finally took a good hard look at myself. I had a reputation as the biggest tyrant in the business. Katie had seen it, too, even before she . . . died. She tried hard to keep me humble." A half-smile played about his lips, then faded abruptly. "She'd always wanted to come . . . back home . . . to raise our family. When I saw that her worst fears were realized, I did what she wanted. Too late, of course," he added with a touch of bitterness.

"So here I am," Cass sighed. "Sometimes I still feel guilty. If I'd just listened to her and come home when she wanted, she'd still be here."

"That's not true," Peyton remonstrated gently. "We don't know when our time to go is."

"That's what I tell myself. But now I can think of Katie as she was, sitting in that silly swing in the elm tree. I can remember that I loved her."

"You're still mourning." Peyton spoke with compassion, then waited for his response.

It could mark the real beginning of their fragile relationship—or the end. Yet she felt nothing but sorrow for Cass's losses: the family that never was, a career that had consumed him, and most important, the woman who'd been his wife, who had kept him in line, who'd left Peyton this complicated, difficult, wonderful man. She'd have liked Katie, she was sure.

But was Cass capable of moving on? He hadn't answered her question. Grief could do funny things to people. Sometimes, instead of honoring the memory and moving ahead, survivors got stuck in the past, mired in the suffering. If Cass were still grieving . . .

"No." Cass's reply was firm when it came. "Katie wouldn't have wanted me to. She'd have been the first to tell me how rotten I've been to myself and to everyone around me."

Peyton inhaled deeply. The fire's heat burned her lungs; the smoke burned her eyes. "But you still hurt."

"The pain is mostly a memory now. But it hurt so much for so long that I didn't ever want to go through it again."

Peyton sat in silence. Cass's last words cut to the heart of his unwillingness to get involved. She'd been right; he *had* detached his heart from the business of living. She simply hadn't suspected the reason why.

Peyton shivered. Would she have had the courage to come as far as Cass had already?

"So now what?" she asked quietly, expecting a firm good-bye.

"I don't know. You scare the hell out of me, that's for sure. You've got a mile-wide stubborn streak and the nerve to question my judgments." Cass laughed, the first laugh since he'd talked to little Jennifer. A bird rustled in the tree above them.

"It's a dirty job, but somebody's got to do it." Her

casual words revealed none of the nervous flutter in her stomach. It was not like Cass to skirt direct questions.

Peyton looked up at his face shining in the combined glow of the fire and the moonlight, and a wave of tenderness and hope filled her heart. She had survived the day with her feelings for Cass intact, stronger, in fact, because she now knew the depth of emotion Cass was capable of. If he could unlock his heart, his love would be the most wondrous event of her life.

And she could give him a new peace. She would never be Katie, but together they could forge something brand new out of desire and shared dreams, something strong, tempered by passion and understanding, something whole and unbroken. If Cass stood by her side, and she by his, they could achieve anything.

The moon ducked behind a cloud, casting a fleeting shadow on Cass's face. Peyton reached up to touch his face with the same intimate gesture he'd used on her. As her fingers connected with his skin, her fears melted. Tonight all that existed were she and Cass. Dreamily, she reached out to him, enfolding his shoulders in her soft arms. He tilted her head toward his and slowly brought his lips down to meet hers, tracing feathery patterns along the edges of her mouth.

The fire might be dying, but not Peyton. She was very much alive. Passion, in the intense aftermath of catharsis, licked her body, making her inch closer and closer to Cass. She emitted a deep, throaty sound as Cass used his tongue to brush pleasure into the skin of her face and neck.

He outlined rich swirls against her skin, alternately using his lips and his tongue until she thought she could endure no more. Peyton guided his mouth back to hers, reveling in the warmth and desire she found in him. They kissed for an eternity, lips on lips, then she welcomed the invasion of his tongue. Her throat was dry, but he brought her precious moisture, and soon she felt the gentle lubrication that told her she was ready for much more.

Tenderly Cass lowered her to the tarp. The earth smelled pungent and fresh, a mixture of dew and leaves and the last of the fire. Above her Peyton could see the moon emerging from a wispy cloud. Cass stretched his full length beside her, pinning her right leg beneath his own and wedging his left hand between her waist and her bottom. Softly he tugged at her turtleneck, easing it out of her trousers and seeking out the warm responsive flesh it had covered.

He paused a moment as if to etch her face permanently on his memory, and Peyton knew he found her beautiful. Then he raised himself on his left side and began to kiss her urgently. His tongue probed and prodded responses she'd never known she could give, and she felt deliciously wanton in his arms. She nudged her leg deeper between his two, delighting in the hardness that spoke eloquently of his need for her.

She answered with a passion of her own. She breathed deeply and brushed her breasts against his hard chest. She gyrated slowly as his left hand caressed her backside, generating a rivulet of dampness that clung to her thighs.

This is not the time, a warning voice cried in her head, but Peyton refused to listen. The tension had been too great this evening, the potential for loss too devastating. All she wanted now was to drown in the sensation of the man beside her.

Cass slipped the turtleneck over her head and dug his fingers into her coppery skin. His hands were warm, eager. Their energy stoked the fire within her. Softly he trailed his hand up, up, up, keeping tempo with the precipitous rise and fall of her chest.

He rested his hand lightly on her breast, the heat of his fingertips burning through the filmy lace of her bra. He waited a moment, two, three, then flipped open the front clasp and released her breasts to the cool night air. The kiss of night made her nipples hard, and Cass cupped his hand over her to warm her, skin against skin.

The heat spread until it suffused her body, settling deep in her bones. It radiated down and inward until she could stand his sweet torture no longer. Cass had readied her for even greater heat, greater passion, and she wanted both. Now.

"You have me at a disadvantage," she murmured throatily.

Shifting her weight, she reached up and neatly unbuttoned his shirt. Pushing it aside, she slid it off his shoulders and banished it to the ground. Then she smoothed her palms along the hard planes of his chest, savoring the springy expanse of hair on her flesh.

The moonlight glinted on Cass's skin, casting light and shadows across the ripples of muscle. She couldn't wait much longer, and she pulled Cass down to meet her. Hard and soft, silver and copper, their bodies played against each other. Cass's hands danced like fireflies on Peyton's skin, teasing her with their hardened edges, convulsing her with his feather-light touch.

Excitement rippled through her, moving outward from her center and lodging in her fingers and toes. This was powerful, hot, and tempting . . . and she was beyond controlling her body's response, even if she wanted to. It had taken over, bathing her in sensation, setting her nerves on fire.

Cass massaged her tenderly, squeezing her breasts.

Just as Peyton thought she'd die from the exquisite blend of pleasure and pain, he lowered his mouth to cool the fever raging there.

Peyton arched upward to meet him. She wanted nothing more than to meld herself to him, to spend a night of passion under the stars. His tongue flickered and pranced, promising a world of ecstasy if only she wanted to travel with him.

"Oh, Cass, that feels so wonderful," she groaned. "I never knew you would feel so good."

She curled her body around to spoon with his, face to face. His manhood pressed against her abdomen, and she knew fervent, unfettered desire. She squirmed to soothe the dull ache between her thighs, but only the pressure of Cass's masculinity brought any relief.

Full to bursting, needing and craving release, Peyton slid her hands over his back, tracing his musculature, tickling him with the lightest of caresses. Then, with newfound boldness, she ran her hands around his waist, slipping in to free Cass from the belt at his hips.

"My God," he muttered, kissing her lips, her ears, her eyelids. "You're driving me crazy. I want you so much."

"I want you, too, Cass."

He buried himself in handfuls of her luxuriant hair and pressed his full weight against her. Peyton welcomed him, welcomed the edgy, unsatisfied need that coursed through her.

She couldn't quite fill her lungs as Cass rolled his full length atop her. She took short, shallow breaths, waiting, waiting.

Her warm breath played on Cass's neck and shoulder, and he shuddered lightly. "Take me away, Peyton," he whispered raggedly. "Take me away and make me forget."

What had he said? A foggy corner of Peyton's brain lurched through the depths of passion and clung to his words. Make him forget? Forget what? Katie? All the pain? The guilt? The reason he'd come back? Her?

She lay still as recognition washed over her; sadness replaced desire. The emptiness between her legs still throbbed, unrelieved.

Cass sought her breast, but this time she denied him. She placed her hands on either side of his face and turned his head towards her.

"No," she said softly, shaking her head. "I don't want you to forget. Not ever. Not Katie, not the pain, not the joy. I want you to remember it all."

"I do remember it," he growled, jerking away from her touch and rolling to his side. "I *live* with it. Every day."

Peyton took a deep breath, her first since their passion had started building. Then another and another. The night had grown colder, and the fire had burned back to a few faint embers. No warmth there.

None from Cass, either. She crossed her arms in front of her, covering herself, trying to stave off the cold.

What could she do? Tonight had been a first step, but it wasn't enough. Cass might be past the worst of the pain of losing Katie, but his heart still lived in the half light of memory, shrouded by guilt, insulated from any new relationship. Safe. From the world. From her.

She wanted him, oh, how she wanted him! But not on those terms. She wouldn't be a means to forget, a substitute, a replacement. She couldn't settle for that, despite the yawning emptiness inside her, the lips bruised by kisses, and the aching memory of Cass's body covering her. She didn't want this kind of inti-

macy until Cass was ready to live in the light of love.
Her love. Theirs.

Cass groaned heavily, and Peyton turned toward him.
He was curled up like a child, and the sight tore at her.
It would have been easy to give in, to take and give
solace. But it wouldn't be fair—not to him and certainly
not to her.

She sat up, still lightheaded, and rearranged her
clothing, pulling on her turtleneck and tucking it in.
She tried to smooth her hair, but it was as unruly as
her heart and refused her attempts to settle it.

Cass lifted himself to a sitting position, fumbled for
his shirt and yanked it on. He didn't bother to button
it. He rose and stamped out the last embers of the fire,
leaving behind only ash. He helped Peyton to her feet
and folded the tarp.

"It's just as well. I can't promise you anything, Peyton," he said plainly. They started walking towards the
house.

"I'm not asking for promises. I just want you to put
the past away and build a new future. Until you do, I
can't—" but she couldn't finish the sentence.

Suddenly she was very tired.

So much had happened today; she'd seen depths to
Cass that she'd only hoped were there. He'd convinced
her that they had a chance. Then she'd slammed against
the stone wall that protected his heart.

That wasn't entirely accurate. Her own fierce determination that their relationship should be built on a
stronger foundation than sympathy had played a role.
But any way she looked at it, she was going home.

Alone.

SIX

By early November, Peyton needed an extended vacation in the state mental hospital. Her projects had tripled since her midweek jaunt to the Pumpkin Show. Cass was waiting for her report on new promotional strategies. Advertising revenues had risen, which translated to more commercials to approve and schedule. And *she* was responsible for "On Air Columbus," as Cass so frequently reminded her. In her spare time, she had to oversee a thousand details for the radio executives' convention. After all, she was the chairman.

The latter had already gobbled a healthy chunk of her time. But it was important—for her confidence and her career. The contacts and business ties she'd strengthen would come in handy when she was ready to make her next move.

All this extra work provided a ready excuse to avoid further intimacy with Cass. Since that evening on his farm, Peyton had taken care not to be alone with him. Their meetings always included other staff members, and the tone was cool and businesslike—numbers, facts, figures. No hint of affection, of pain, or of shared experiences colored their exchanges.

Strange warm currents still threaded their way through her heart whenever she glimpsed him striding about the station, powerful and in command. But Peyton kept her thoughts and emotions tightly controlled. She was at too much risk of losing the rest of her heart to Cass.

And that was dangerous. She had goals and ambitions, a fact she ought to keep in mind. Cass had left the very place she wanted to go: New York. In the prime of his career, Cass had thrown it all away.

Even if they could work out the complexities of their relationship, could she be content to spend the rest of her working life in Columbus? Would she handicap her career by foregoing the number one market, forever unable to match others' experience? Would she always be just a little bit less than Cass, standing at the edge of his shadow?

How could she ever hope to buy her own station without the fearless confidence that came with conquering the challenges and demands of New York?

And there was Cass himself. *He* had to come to terms with the question of loving again, by himself. It all boiled down to that. She could decide he was worth abandoning every dream she'd ever had, but if Cass couldn't make room for her in his life, they had no future.

Peyton winced at the thought, then let the truth of it settle around her like dust. She cared for Cass, deeply. But she had to protect herself.

So she feigned indifference and worked long, hard hours to keep from thinking about—or seeing—him. The work seemed meaningless, but it was plentiful— and preferable to the insistent want of Cass, when she knew it might not ever happen.

Peyton sighed with frustration and bounced her pencil eraser restlessly on the edge of the desk. Suddenly the menu choices for the association banquets seemed trivial. Who cared if they ate beef tips or chicken?

She glanced at her to-do list. It was still as long as when she'd written it. The pencil slipped from her fingers and hit the floor. The tip snapped, and with it, the calm facade Peyton had maintained the past two weeks. She rose and pulled her coat from the hook on her door. She had to get out, get some air, calm down. There was too much to do and not enough help. And always, at the heart of it, was Cass.

She picked up the phone and called Sally.

"I've got to get out of here!" Peyton said, not even identifying herself when Sally answered. Sally, bless her, never missed a trick.

"Meet you at City Center? Twenty minutes?"

"Yeah. Thanks, Sal!"

Peyton hiked the six blocks through the chill, dank November air. The sky was white and cheerless, the yellow sunlight of fall having given way to the blue-white ice of winter. The wind cut mercilessly through her coat, but the cold kept her mind off heartache and confusion.

"How've you been, Sal?" Peyton hugged her just inside the main mall entrance.

Sally flipped a thumbs down sign. "Lousy. Still no steady work. The job market's tight."

Peyton shivered, forcing the winter chill from her body. "But you've got so much experience!"

"Lots of on-air experience," she corrected. "But the fact is, radio personalities have to be young, to appeal to kids. I sound like a middle-aged grandma, so the best work I'm getting is voice-overs for Geritol and Depends!"

Peyton shook her head in disbelief. "Sal, I'm so sorry. I never dreamed you'd have trouble finding work."

"Neither did I. But I'd been with 'FKN so long, I'd forgotten what it's like out here."

They moved into the glass-enclosed mall and sauntered past the bright window displays.

"I should have fought harder to keep you," Peyton said with regret. "You did such a good job reassuring me that I just assumed you'd come out on top."

"Times change." Sally shrugged. "I don't resent it, but I sure wish I'd worked in sales or administration or production . . . Even three months of experience would have been useful."

Peyton stopped mid-stride. "Are you serious?" she asked.

"Heck, yes. Look, I could probably get an on-air job in Cincinnati or Cleveland, but my life is here: the kids, Jack, the house. A little management experience could probably get me a decent job here, too."

Peyton made a few lightning calculations, then spoke again. "What would you say to coming back?"

"To 'FKN?" Sally sounded incredulous.

"I'm going crazy. I need help with the day-to-day stuff until this conference is over."

"I appreciate the offer, but don't you want someone who knows what they're doing?"

"It's not that hard." She put her arm around Sally's shoulder. "And I trust you."

"Won't the staff resent your bringing me in?"

"They know you. And it's only for a few months. It doesn't make sense to give somebody added responsibility, only to take it away. This solves all the problems—you get experience, I get help, the staff doesn't get run over roughshod."

They entered a store and maneuvered around the sparkling glass counters that displayed gloves and scarves and perfume.

"What about Cass?"

"What about him?" Peyton tried to keep her voice nonchalant.

Sally shot her a curious look. "He fired me. How's he going to feel about your rehiring me behind his back?"

"Who cares?"

"Uh-oh. This sounds personal."

Peyton sighed. "It is. And very complicated." Haltingly, she told Sally the story Cass had recited by the fire, how he'd lost his wife and his soul.

"You sound awfully down about this," Sally said quietly.

"I am," Peyton admitted. "It's a lot of things: the conference, all these new responsibilities, my career . . ."

"And Cass."

Peyton nodded. "I've never felt this way about a man, Sally. In all the years I've been dating, no man has ever made me look forward to each day like Cass does. He challenges me, he excites me, he even puts a spark in my status quo. I think I'm in love with him, and I don't know how to make him believe in me. So I avoid him."

"You're afraid of failing," Sally said simply. "Love is very risky. But if you don't take risks, well, you might not fail, but you surely won't succeed, either."

Peyton thought for a moment. "I was ready to hate Cass when I met him. God knows, he wreaked havoc with the station and the people. But somehow he got past my defenses and under my skin." She sighed again.

"And if he can't learn to love you, you're going to get hurt. But love, real love, is worth that risk."

"Too bad I'm such a coward," Peyton said morosely.

"You did pick a particularly tough case," Sally observed. "But Peyton, if life's taught me anything in fifty years, it's that you have to go after what you want. The only question is, what do you want?"

"What do I really want?" Peyton thought aloud. "A few months ago it was all so clear: a couple more years here, then New York, then my own station. Marriage and kids—someday. Now it's muddier. If Cass were ready . . ."

Peyton shook her head firmly. "No. He left New York to get on with his life. I still have to get there. We're pulling in opposite directions."

"Given that fact," Sally prompted, "what do you want?"

Peyton stopped in the middle of the aisle to deliberate, oblivious to the early lunchtime crowds whose way she was blocking. Sally waited patiently, waving the other shoppers around them.

What *did* she want? Her career ambitions no longer held the fascination they once had; only recently she would have gloried in the myriad details and long hours of work her job demanded. Now, she was unable to keep a thousand balls juggling; they seemed hollow, empty. So if not an ambitious career, what?

Nothing held the promise that she and Cass did: what they might be—could be—together, if she found the courage to show him.

Cass knew fear, rightfully so. The past had been cruel to him. But *she* was afraid of the future, afraid of the possibility that she and Cass might not be able to find their way. And they wouldn't if she didn't open herself to him, offer him the honesty of her feelings. It would be hard, it carried risk, and it held the power to make her life—their life—full and rich.

If she didn't try, she didn't deserve him.

"I want Cass," Peyton said distinctly. "I want a chance with him. My career can come later, or maybe all my ambitions will change, but I want my future to include Cass."

Sally and Peyton started walking along the aisle again. Peyton hugged her decision to her, knowing she'd taken a big step. There was no turning back. The future, and Cass, lay ahead.

"Are you going to tell him?" Sally asked softly.

Peyton considered the question. "Not yet," she replied. "I needed to make that decision for me. He's not ready to make that decision for himself."

She paused at a counter and picked up an Ohio State toboggan cap. She ran her fingers over the soft wool, tracing the patterns of the scarlet and gray stripes.

"I'll take it slowly. But I'm going to show him that I care. I think I'll start with this." She handed the cap and a ten dollar bill to the salesclerk.

"I can't believe it," Sally teased. "A Wolverine buying an OSU hat!"

"It'll loosen his image around the office. Who can be scared of a guy in Buckeye gear?"

"Nobody around the station, that's for sure. Not with 'FKN broadcasting the football games this season."

"Exactly," she said, and then the idea struck her. "What a great idea! It's a perfect excuse to get together. I'll invite him to the football game this week. If he doesn't want to sit in the press box, I'm sure I can get my hands on a couple of tickets. Either way . . ."

"Peyton, you devil!" Sally laughed. "Cass isn't going to stand a chance."

Peyton looked at her friend seriously. "Thanks for straightening me out. You see how much I need you?"

She took the package from the salesclerk and turned to Sally. "I want you to come to work tomorrow. I'll let people know you're coming back to help out, and we'll get started first thing in the morning."

"You're sure?"

Peyton nodded. "Absolutely. Aren't you always telling me you've got to have faith?"

Sally grinned sheepishly.

"Well, take your own advice." She leaned over and gave her friend another quick hug.

"I guess it beats pounding the pavement. And a little more experience can't hurt." Sally pulled on her gloves and grinned. "See you tomorrow, boss."

Cass stared out at the white sky from the picture window in his office. He'd forgotten how bleak November was in Ohio. Well, today certainly matched his mood. He hadn't had a moment alone with Peyton for weeks, and it had been damnably difficult to concentrate on anything without her.

Which scared him. He'd come home to gain control of the man he'd become, not to fall in love! He never wanted to love again. He never wanted to go through what he'd endured when Katie died. Not ever.

But Peyton was changing that, slowly, a small step at a time. Every day he saw more clearly that he'd been right to come back, right to try to remake himself into someone human. It was working. He could feel it.

Telling Peyton about Katie and his fears had somehow exorcised much of the pain and bitterness he'd carried these five years. The past few days had brought a balm of peace. It had been a long time coming, and Peyton had brought him there. Not that he was home free. He had a lot of unlearning to do, breaking free of the old patterns of privacy and pain, the deeply ingrained habit of secrecy. But he had to try. For himself—and for Peyton.

But he couldn't try without her, and she'd been so busy lately that he wondered if she weren't consciously avoiding him.

She'd been working far too hard. Even in his worst days he hadn't put in the kinds of hours Peyton had recently. She needed some time off—and he needed to see her. How to accomplish that was the question.

The sharp rap at the door broke his reverie. He turned from the window and called "Come in" as Peyton slid in through the half-opened door and closed it behind her. The day had just taken a turn for the better.

"Peyton," he said warmly. "Where have you been keeping yourself? I haven't seen you alone," his voice lingered longingly over the word, "in days."

"I've been busy, boss man," she replied archly.

If only he knew how the sound of his voice made her tremble! She had been crazy to think she could just forget about Cass. Three seconds in his presence and she was as giddy as a schoolgirl, and more optimistic than she'd been in months. Ready or not, he would be hers. She would be his. Together, they would reconcile all their goals and ambitions. They had to. Because she loved this complicated, sexy man.

"Maybe we need an assistant program director around here," Cass suggested.

"Your wish is my command," Peyton responded, not believing her luck. She couldn't have contrived such an opening if she'd written the whole conversation herself. "I just asked Sally Ashton to come back for a few weeks to help out."

Cass narrowed his eyes sharply. "That's bad pol—"

He broke off, spoke again more quietly. "I don't think that's a good idea."

"I'm snowed under, the staff already knows her, and she needs the work. It's ideal."

"It's temporary," Cass countered.

She nodded. "Just until the conference is over. But if I don't have help, you'll never see me. No one will. I'll go nuts and you'll have to lock me away. . . ." Her voice trailed off, and Cass smiled.

Peyton relaxed a fraction. She'd passed the first hurdle. Now to the next step, the first in her all-out assault for his love.

"I've got a surprise for you." She held out the bag with the stocking hat.

"Oh?" He let his fingers stray across Peyton's as he reached for the bag, and that slight touch sent butterflies scrambling in her stomach. She took a quick breath to steady herself. If she weren't careful, he'd know the truth from her body alone. He wouldn't need words to learn how she felt.

It's too soon, she told herself firmly. *Slow down, take things easy. Give it time, give him time . . .*

"A Buckeye hat!" Cass exclaimed. "What an odd surprise coming from you!"

"Not so odd. I *do* teach there, you know. I thought you could wear it to the game next Saturday." Seeing his blank look, she added, "With me. I thought we could keep our eye on the broadcast booth."

"And drive the play-by-play and color commentators crazy? That booth is barely big enough for the two of them, let alone us. I have a better idea."

The butterflies swarmed furiously, tumbling about inside Peyton, sending little shivers of anticipation through her.

"Let's get out of Columbus altogether. You've been working too hard."

"No protest on that score!" she said wryly.

He furrowed his brow in thought and ran his tongue over his upper teeth and over his lips. The sight of it made those butterflies in Peyton's stomach dance and skitter even more wildly. The things his tongue could do to her!

"I'll pick you up on Saturday at nine. Wear something warm and a pair of comfortable shoes."

"Where are we going?"

"It's a surprise. I can give as well as get them, you know." His eyes twinkled with ill-concealed glee. "I'll tell you this much. Where we're going I can wear my new hat."

"Okay," she agreed, savoring the prickling sensation on the nape of her neck. Let him surprise her. This was the way she wanted it to be, getting excited about small events to be shared. They had plenty of time.

"I have to go. I have tons to do," she said, actually anxious to get back to her desk. "I can't wait to see you in that hat." She blew him a kiss and slipped out the door.

"So where *are* we going?" Peyton asked excitedly as she nestled in the front seat of Cass's Jeep on Saturday. She was comfortable in an old pair of jeans and a plaid flannel shirt. Her hightop sneakers covered two pairs of socks, and a down vest and mittens ensured she wouldn't suffer from the cool fall air.

Cass smiled indulgently. One of the things he liked best about Peyton was her unbridled enthusiasm for everything. "Not so fast. It's still a surprise. You have to enjoy the drive first."

"The drive will be more interesting if I know where I'm headed."

"Sorry. You'll just have to wait."

"Rat!" She folded her arms over her chest and faked a convincing pout for a few seconds. Then she changed the subject. "You promised you'd wear the Ohio State hat. Where is it?"

"In back. I don't need it in the car."

"Oh, yes, you do." Before he had a chance to put the car in gear, Peyton fished in the back and brought forth the hat. "Put it on or I'll put it on for you," she threatened, laughing.

"Try it," he dared.

Peyton stretched the cap between her hands and tried to cram it on Cass's head. She got it perched at a cockeyed angle as Cass wrapped his hands around her wrists in self-defense. Spasms of laughter rocked them both as Cass surveyed himself in the rearview mirror.

"It's designed for warmth, not fashion," he observed dryly. "It'll be great when we get to the—" He stopped short, unwilling to spoil Peyton's surprise.

"When we get where?"

"Never mind!"

"Trust me, Cass."

"Never!"

Peyton thought she detected a shadow cross Cass's face. The conversation was suddenly cutting too close to the real issue between them. Cass must have thought so, too, because he dropped her hands and leaned over to kiss her quickly and soundly, as if to reassure her.

His lips were dry and smooth against the soft pink film of her lip gloss. It was just one brief touch, but it told her volumes about Cass's feelings. There was an energy, a controlled passion brewing beneath the surface of the morning's silly antics. The fleeting intimacy of his kiss made Peyton realize that Cass had missed her as much as she'd missed him. He might not want to love ever again, but he'd have a hard time preventing it.

Cass handled the narrow county roads expertly as he drove from the flat plains of central Ohio to the gently rolling hills further south. The fields that a few weeks ago had been filled with ripening wheat were now harvested, leaving behind only stubble to cover the rich earth. A few small pumpkins sat unclaimed in their patches. Peyton unzipped her window about an inch to enjoy the crisp morning air and the distant smoky scent of burning leaves.

"I love the fall," she said. "The weather's right, the land looks right, my clothes are right. It's the best time of the year."

"It's not really fall until after we've been where we're going," Cass said. "Not until we've eaten apples from this year's harvest and drunk the cider from the old press, and hiked in the woods . . . Then it's really fall."

"What *are* you talking about?" Peyton asked.

"Give me five minutes. You'll see."

A few moments later, Peyton saw the sign that read "Laurelville, pop. 591." Cass followed the two lane main street past a small diner and a school before pulling up beside a white barn. On the side of the barn in faded letters were the words "The Apple Barrel."

"The apples!" Peyton said in recognition.

"Best apples in the state. We can get just about every variety—Delicious, Winesaps, Jonathans, Staymans. And their cider is fantastic."

The sweet smell of ripe apples, honey and cider assailed Peyton's nostrils as they entered the old store. A kerosene heater stood in one corner, but the heat didn't radiate far in the drafty building. Peyton stamped her feet to get her blood moving.

"What can I do for you?" asked the grizzled older man as he shuffled over from a chair near the heater.

"Hi, Mr. Jones. We need a bag of apples, a couple of gallons of cider, and a jar of honey—with comb."

"Do I know you?" the man asked quizzically, looking closely at Cass. "You seem to know me."

"Cass Sloane, Mr. Jones. It's been a long time."

The man scratched his thinning hair for a minute in thought. "Of course! I remember. You're Mac's little boy. How is your father?"

"Pretty well. He's retired now, living in Florida. He comes back in the summer to visit."

"Tell him I said hello. Tell him to come give me a hand when he's home."

"I will."

"You go choose your apples. They're all bagged up over on that table. I'll get your cider and honey." He disappeared behind a refrigerator locker door.

"I'm amazed," Peyton said. "We're in the middle of nowhere and you know this fellow!"

"We used to come down here a lot when I was little," Cass replied. "I belong here. These are my roots." He walked over to the table stacked with peck and half peck bags of apples. "What do you like, Peyton? Tart or sweet?"

"Tart."

"I like 'em sour myself," Cass agreed. "Much more flavor that way." He looked at several bags before selecting a peck of Staymans. The fruit was a rich red color, round and firm, and Peyton could almost taste the luscious juice running down her throat.

The older man returned with two plastic jugs of cider

and a pot of honey. "That all you need?" he asked laconically.

"I think so, Mr. Jones," Cass answered. "What do we owe you?"

Cass counted out the bills and waved good-bye to his father's friend. As they loaded the back of the truck with their purchases, Peyton selected a small, perfectly round apple and hid it in her vest pocket.

"I saw that," Cass said as she climbed in the front seat. "Greedy thing. You can't even wait till we're on the road before you start eating."

"It looked too good to pass up," she confessed, pulling the apple out. She bit into it, and the cold fruit tasted sour-sweet and refreshing. The apple was juicy, and little drops of the sticky stuff ran down from the corners of her mouth.

She licked her lips, catching the last of the juice. She handed the apple to Cass. It was too delicious not to share. "Mmmm! It's wonderful! You've got to try it!"

"I've got a better way to try it," he said slyly. He took a large bite of the apple, holding it halfway in his mouth with his front teeth. Then he reached over to claim Peyton's mouth with his own, inviting her to share the tender bit of fruit with him.

Peyton opened her mouth to accept his gift. The morsel slid easily between her teeth, and she chewed slowly, eyes closed, savoring the mixture of apple and Cass. She swallowed and wanted more. When she crossed the short distance between their lips, she found Cass had finished his bite, too. Only his lips awaited, moist and fruity.

She inhaled the heady fragrance as she nibbled his lower lip, sucking the last of the flavor from it. Then she began to taste Cass himself, and she grew warm.

She parted her lips to allow her tongue to explore recesses of Cass's mouth, the mouth that had taught her so much about passion and pleasure.

Cass responded with a groan and forcefully took possession of her mouth. He wrapped her ponytail around his free hand and pulled her as close as the bucket seats would allow. After several long seconds, she opened her eyes and whispered, "Wow! They grow some kind of apples in Ohio."

Cass reluctantly released her and handed back the rest of the apple. "You'd better finish it alone," he said. "Another bite like that and we'll never get where we're going."

"Not to mention the scandal we'd cause here in the center of town!"

Peyton felt alive, whole, invigorated. That kiss had connected with something vital deep within her, and she could feel renewed affection and courage course through her body. She and Cass would be all right.

A short while later, Cass pulled the Jeep into Hocking Hills State Park.

"Cass, it's beautiful," Peyton said, clambering down from her seat. "Even from the parking lot you can see miles of trees, all decked out in their fall finery!"

"It gets better. Once you've hiked a mile or so, you'll really see Mother Nature." He hoisted a small day pack from the backseat and stocked it with cider and apples.

"I'm ready. Let's go!"

The trail was easy, sloping gently downward. The earth, with its blanket of early fallen leaves, had been tamped solid by the hordes of fall hikers who came to these Appalachian foothills to enjoy the change of season. Peyton thought she had never seen anything quite so stark and yet so lovely as this place. Sheer walls of sandstone rose around her, taller than all but the oldest trees. Somewhere nearby roared a waterfall, but the rest of the woods were silent.

Peyton breathed deeply, drinking in the simple natural beauty. The earth was redolent with the smell of decaying leaves and fallen nuts, a rich musty smell that promised survival through the winter and renewal in the spring. Through the half empty tree branches Peyton could see the patchy blue of the Ohio sky.

"It's so remarkably beautiful," she whispered, reluctant to disturb the chapel-like stillness. "I never knew this was here."

"It is marvelous," Cass agreed. "It lacks the upstart grandeur of, say, the Grand Tetons, but it's been around a lot longer. Wait til you see the caves."

"Caves?"

"That's what I like best about this place. You'll see."

They walked on, talking little. They had no need for words. The intimacy with nature had created a mirroring intimacy between them. Peyton reached out and squeezed Cass's hand briefly in gratitude. Cass squeezed back, and when Peyton moved to drop it, he wouldn't let her go. Her hand stayed cradled in his, and the touch of his strong fingers twined around hers sent little shivers scurrying up her back.

"Cold?" he asked.

"Oh, no," she said softly. "Not cold at all."

They scrambled down the side of the final hill, and Peyton stopped still at the sight before her. A small lagoon stood placidly, the water broken at one end by a small waterfall. The rock surrounding the pool towered around them, creating an overhang that suggested a cave.

"It's wonderful!"

"I used to come here as a kid. It never seemed like fall until we'd made the annual trek to Old Man's Cave. I haven't been back for a long time."

"I'm glad you brought me," Peyton said sincerely. It was a good sign, Cass sharing himself and his past this way. "Why is it called Old Man's Cave?"

"The story goes that there was an old man who made his home here. It was after the Civil War, and he must have been accused of some terrible crimes, because he was a fugitive. He escaped and staked his claim here in the hills. The government never came after him, and he died here, a bitter old hermit."

"How sad! That war did such terrible things to people. The poor man missed out on all the joy in life."

Cass looked at Peyton oddly, and Peyton realized that he could easily understand the old man's decision. She lifted her hand, still holding his, and pressed them to her cheek.

"Don't you go getting any such ideas. Running away is no answer," she whispered.

"I already ran away," he said, looking straight down into Peyton's eyes and the sight of his hand clasped against her face.

"How can you say that, Cass?"

"It's true. I ran away from New York, and I'm still running away from love. I find you fascinating, but I can't seem to trust myself."

What now? Peyton thought. *I'll only scare him if I tell him how I feel.* "Nobody said we have to make lifelong decisions right this minute," she said, smiling warmly. "We could just enjoy today."

"We could." They walked along in silence for a few minutes along the edge of the water.

"The old man had a lot to enjoy." Cass gestured

broadly with his free arm. "The changing seasons, the birds' music, the serenity. It could be enough."

"It couldn't ever be enough," Peyton protested. "There's too much of life to savor. I want to work, fall in love, get married, have kids. . . . It wouldn't be enough for you, either," she added shrewdly, suddenly realizing that Cass was searching for clues about her feelings. He wanted to know how much of her heart she'd risk for him. He couldn't know that she'd already decided he was worth rearranging every dream she'd ever dreamed.

If only he could let go enough to dream some of his own. Dreams that included her by his side. Peyton sighed softly. This loving business was far more complicated than it should be.

"You're probably right. I'd go stark raving mad out here for too long," Cass said. "I need action and a day-to-day job."

You need me, Peyton thought, but she didn't voice her opinion. It was still better to go slowly.

They hiked up a sandstone stairway, carved by man and worn smooth by generations of hikers seeking the solace of nature. At the top of the stairs not far from the path was a small wooded grove. Cass stopped and unslung his backpack.

"What would you say to a little snack?" he asked cheerfully. He appeared to have banished his earlier moments of introspection.

"Want to start with the apples?" Peyton teased.

"What would your mother say to starting with dessert?"

"She'd say she raised a daughter who knew what she wanted."

Cass took a small blanket from the pack and spread it on the ground, then pulled out the food. The exercise had given Peyton quite an appetite. Cass had brought crusty rolls, piled high with ham and cheese, carrot sticks and soft oatmeal cookies, plus apples and cool cider to wash it all down. Peyton thought she'd never eaten food quite so good.

"You pack a great picnic," she said as she wiped her mouth clean of mustard and cookie crumbs.

"You missed a little," Cass said, reaching across the blanket with a napkin to touch the corner of her mouth. He dabbed the last bits of lunch away. Then, as if unwilling to leave her, he dropped the napkin and brushed up a stray hair that had escaped from her ponytail. He traced the line of her cheekbone with his fingertips. Each touch sent a new thrill down Peyton's back. She wanted him to keep touching her, but now he was moving his hand away. Unthinking, she pulled him back towards her. She closed her eyes and kissed him. It was a long kiss, profoundly feminine, and it sent Cass reeling.

"Peyton," he protested deep in his throat. But Peyton would hear none of it. A deep warm glow had kindled within her, a glow she wanted to share with Cass. Heedless of the possible consequences and her previous vows of caution forgotten, she put her arms around his neck and kissed him again, roundly, fully, with all the passion her woman's body could bring to bear. She had to make him understand how she felt.

Slowly she trailed her hand down the scratchy wool of Cass's hunter's jacket, feeling the rapid rising of his chest as he breathed. Then she worked the buttons of the jacket open with her left hand and slid her fingers into the warm safe haven under his coat.

Beneath the soft napped chamois shirt, Peyton could feel Cass's muscled chest. She traced his sinews with her index finger and lazily circled his nipple. It stood at attention, testimony to her ability to make Cass want her as much as she wanted him.

"Peyton," Cass groaned again. "Not . . ."

"Shh," she breathed, silencing him with another kiss. This time she probed with her tongue, exploring all the contours of his moist mouth. She slid over his smooth teeth, then urged them open with a flick of her demanding tongue.

The glowing ember inside Peyton began to build, suffusing her with a heat she'd thought impossible this late in the year. Blood pumped furiously through her body, blocking all sensations but those she was creating with Cass.

He was responding now. He wrapped one arm around her shoulder and worked the other down her turtleneck onto the soft skin of her neck. Peyton shuddered gently as his cool hand connected with her flesh, but it was a pleasurable shudder. He began to knead her skin expertly, seeming to know instinctively what would feel right and bring the best combination of delight and sensation.

His mouth played on hers in short intensive bursts. Then he settled into a slower rhythm, matching the strokes of her tongue with his own. He reached up to undo the clasp that held her hair and braided his fingers through the waves tumbling around his hands. Then slowly he caressed her face with his thumb.

He brought it down Peyton's face to her throat, stretching the neck of her shirt to reveal the hollow at its base. He rested there lightly, and Peyton could feel her pulse throbbing beneath him. He inclined his head and kissed her neck, twice, three times. He nibbled the exposed skin gently as his hand descended to unbutton her flannel shirt and tug it loose from her jeans. Triumphantly he cupped her breast. Peyton trembled, her senses heightened anew.

Cass massaged the softness of Peyton's breast. He teased her nipple erect, molding it taut between his fingers. In contrast the mound surrounding it stood pliant, waiting, needing.

He fondled and caressed her, stroking her skin until she was beyond ready for release. She moaned, reaching into his shirt to run her fingers through the wiry hair of his chest. She ached to feel him next to her, on top of her, deep inside her. She longed to give him the complete gift of her love.

"Cass, oh Cass," she whispered. "I want you to make love to me."

Almost imperceptibly, Cass slowed the tempo of his caresses, as if to give Peyton time to change her mind. He came to a stop, one hand lying lightly on her abdomen and the other supporting her shoulder.

"Why did you stop?" Peyton cried, hurt. Was it possible that Cass didn't feel the same way? His body hadn't lied about his wanting her. She was sure of that. "I didn't want you to stop."

"Shh," he said, cocking his head. "I thought I heard something."

Then Peyton heard it, too. A rustle of leaves to their left indicated an animal of some sort. Bright eyes peered at them through the trees. Then, from the trail below them came the sound of human voices. Spooked, the creature turned and ran.

The voices came closer, wafting up from the same stairs Peyton and Cass had used. Regretfully, Peyton pulled away from Cass.

"I feel like a teenager who's been caught out past curfew," she said sheepishly, buttoning her shirt and tucking it in.

Quietly they gathered up the picnic remains and packed it in the backpack. They rose in time to greet, with feigned heartiness, a small group of hikers led by a park ranger. Then they began the trek back to the Jeep.

"I meant what I said back there." Peyton's voice broke the stillness. "I want you to make love to me."

Cass stopped, turned to face Peyton, and enfolded her in his arms. "I want it, too," he said simply. "But not yet. I'm not ready. I don't trust my feelings enough. And the last thing I want is to hurt you by making love with you and discovering that I can't go through with it or I regret it. I want to go slowly."

Peyton thought for a moment. She probably ought to feel humiliated that she'd thrown herself at him and been rejected, but her only emotion was relief. Her first instinct, to go slowly, had been vindicated. Cass agreed with her. They would do just that: take it slowly. There was plenty of time.

They arrived back in the parking lot before dusk and settled in for the two hour drive back. They chatted about inconsequential things, bantering back and forth as they'd grown accustomed to doing. As Cass rounded the corner to her street, he said, "It's been a lovely day. I'm glad you joined me."

"So am I," she replied. "Of course, I have that much more work I have to get done tomorrow."

"I'd tell you not to work too hard, but it wouldn't do any good," Cass said, pulling the car into her driveway. He left the motor running as he got out to open Peyton's door and walk her to the door.

On the stoop, Cass kissed her good night. It was a gentle kiss, with little of the fire and passion that had caught them up earlier. But it bespoke a friendship that could weather a storm.

"Seriously," he said, turning to go. "Don't wear yourself out tomorrow. I'd like my favorite program director to have breakfast with me on Monday."

She smiled shyly. "I think that can be arranged. Thanks for a wonderful day."

SEVEN

The telephone on Peyton's desk buzzed insistently.

"Mr. Sloane wants to see you," the station's secretary said. "Immediately!"

"I'll be right up." Peyton put the receiver back in its cradle and pulled a manila folder out of the desk drawer. Best to be armed with all the evidence. She'd been expecting this encounter for a couple of weeks; she was only surprised it hadn't come sooner.

"He's in rare form," the secretary warned as Peyton knocked on Cass's door.

"Good morning," Peyton said. She would *not* be nervous. She'd done everything according to protocol. She closed the door behind her and crossed the room to the leather sofa.

Cass rose from behind his desk and strode over to the couch. Peyton took a deep breath to steady herself as she watched Cass's imposing figure approach. The past few weeks had passed between them in a glow of friendship and affection. They'd eaten breakfast together in cozy pancake houses, worked late, and grown more comfortable together. The chill gray of November had been warmed by the smoldering embers of their feelings, feelings eager to burst into flames of passion.

But personal sentiment aside, he was still able to inspire professional awe. She felt her confidence flicker.

"Peyton," he began without preliminaries. "What's this I hear about 'Top Kid' going into reruns?"

Here it comes, she thought. *He's finally found the memo.*

She'd convinced him in one of their marathon working nights that a live audience, with a regular cast of youngsters, would broaden the show's appeal. And to get that audience, "Top Kid" would be going on the road—taping in the schools and community centers around town. In its new format, the show would air both Saturday and Sunday, still early, but with twice the exposure.

"It's true," she replied. "The staff needed the extra time to get the details worked out for taking 'Top Kid' out of the studio. And since it's not economical for three full-time staffers to be out every week, I've reassigned some of the interns. But it takes time to train them to handle the engineering on location. Reruns seemed the most logical way to handle our time needs."

"You know my stand on reruns." Cass's face was dark.

"How could I forget?" Peyton's tone was dry. "Cass, it was the only way. If we continued to produce new shows *and* tried to get the ideas in place, it'd be Easter before we'd be broadcasting the new 'Top Kid.' That's too long."

"Peyton, the purpose of radio is to be fresh and different three hundred and sixty-five days a year!" Cass glowered.

"That's a wonderful goal to strive for, but let's look at reality. We have a chance to influence all kinds of kids—expose them to radio, to a possible career, to positive role models. In another two weeks we'll be doing that."

"Nothing is worth reruns." Cass's voice was flat.

"They're not 'reruns.' They're composites of several shows broadcast over the past two and a half years." She did some lightning calculations in her mind. "I have over thirty-two hundred minutes of 'Top Kid' on tape. I'm reusing ten percent."

Cass sat down beside her. "You should've discussed this with me."

Peyton looked at him quizzically. "I did." She opened the manila folder and pulled out a typed memo. "I sent this more than two weeks ago," she said, handing him the paper. "When I didn't hear from you, I assumed you agreed." Of course, she'd fully expected him to send her a reverberating "No!" but this was not the time to bring *that* up.

"What *is* this?" Cass said incredulously, scanning the paper. There, in neat black and white, were all of Peyton's plans: dates, times and personnel. "Why haven't I seen this?"

"I don't know." She kept her voice calm and innocent, but inside she experienced a fleeting moment of glee at catching Cass in a human error. He did everything so meticulously, so thoroughly. She welcomed the fact that he could make mistakes. It made him seem more genuine. "It's not on your desk, is it?"

"Couldn't possibly be," he muttered. But he got up from the couch and walked over to his "in" box. Peyton resisted the temptation to follow him and instead allowed herself the luxury of enjoying his rear view.

Gray flannel trousers hugged his lean hips, gracefully

outlining every curve of his buttocks. His black sweater did the same to his back, hinting broadly at the power and strength of his torso. Involuntarily, Peyton remembered the feel of his arms around her, the sweet sensation of his firm chest against her cheek. Her heart was pounding and color had crept to her face before she could train her thoughts away. She wasn't sure how much of it was memory and how much of it was nerves.

"Found it," Cass said. "Looks like it got clipped to some other stuff by mistake." He returned to the sofa and began to read the memo carefully. Reactions flashed across his face, and Peyton felt the heat of anger and the cool chill of logic do battle as he read paragraph after paragraph.

Finally he looked away from the memo to her. She braced herself for his inevitable comments.

"Very good."

"You agree with me?" She couldn't keep the surprise out of her voice.

"I'd still like to know why you didn't discuss this with me verbally, but, yes, your reasoning is sound. You *are* the PD; it's your job to make these decisions."

"I put it in writing because you want everything in writing. Something about 'stockholders' and 'covering your anatomy,' I think." She smiled faintly.

"And a memo was far easier than facing me with the prospects of, uh, encore performances, as you so euphemistically put it." His tone was hard, but Peyton detected the barest hint of humor in his eyes. She breathed a silent sigh of relief.

"We haven't gotten any complaints," she teased. "And our audience for 'Top Kid' changes every year. There are hundreds of kids who've never heard these programs."

Cass sat back against the sofa and laced his fingers

behind his head. He stared across the room at the landscape oil that hung on the opposite wall. The handsome chrome clock behind them ticked inexorably—seconds, minutes. Peyton's relief began to evaporate.

Finally he spoke. "I wish you'd trusted me enough to be able to discuss this decision with me."

Peyton caught her breath sharply, recognizing the truth of his statement. For all her talk of trust, she hadn't had the nerve to confide her plans to him. She'd stuck to the letter of the law, but violated its spirit. They'd worked together day and night for weeks, and she hadn't offered him the courtesy he gave her every night when he used her program ideas. Trust. She shrank down into the soft leather, suddenly appalled at her own actions.

What am I supposed to say? she thought. *He's absolutely right.* Cass's sorrowful gaze bore into her like a diamond cutter's tool, chipping away the shards of her confidence and sending them flowing through her bloodstream like ice cubes.

"I understand all your reasons, and I agree with you, but I still don't much care for reruns. Can you push this ahead any faster?" he asked.

"Not without more hands. And I don't think I can reassign anyone else. I love this show, but it's not economical. Even at two hours per week, it doesn't bring in the revenue to warrant more help. We both know that."

"Peyton," he said, taking her hands in his own. She tried to snatch them away. She wasn't worthy of his understanding. But his grip was too strong. The heat from his fingers burned at first, then slowly it thawed the ice flowing through her veins.

She didn't understand his behavior. He'd just told her he was disappointed in her, and now he was holding her hands as if trying to soften the blow. He seemed to be trying to integrate their personal and professional relationships, and Peyton wasn't at all sure she wanted that. Not yet.

"Peyton," he repeated. "If you need another pair of hands, I'll help." At her incredulous look, he continued, "I want 'Top Kid' to succeed, too. The more successful it is, the more credit we both get. I just don't want the new to come at the expense of the old."

Peyton pulled a hand loose from Cass's. Anxiously, she pushed her hair back with her fingers, tousling it. She had to clear her mind of the jumble of images and thoughts that clamored for attention.

"You'd help?" she asked softly.

"I'm a pretty good engineer. And I can make phone calls, drive the van, and practice crowd control on the audience. I'm talented."

Peyton smiled weakly, some of her natural optimism returning. "And modest, too."

"It's only becoming to such a Renaissance man as myself."

"You're impossible!"

"And lovable?"

"Sometimes." Nervously, she ran her hand through her hair again. Cass followed suit, his large hand smoothing the rich auburn waves Peyton had disturbed. A small chill of awareness skipped down her neck. His fingers were still warm, and Peyton could feel their heat radiating, heightening her sense of him.

Cass brought his thumb down to rest on her cheek. His eyes no longer blazed with hurt. Now they glowed with what Peyton read as respect and admiration, and she felt her confusion spiral. Her body was sending her one message, her mind at least two others. She had to learn not only to let Cass trust her, but also to do as he asked and trust him—professionally and emotionally. It was a lot to ask.

"This is so hard," she whispered. "How do we learn to trust each other?"

"Time," Cass said simply. His thumb traced down the smooth skin of Peyton's face to her chin, then down her neck to her throat. Peyton couldn't breathe. Every nerve fiber tingled with anticipation, an anticipation she dreaded. He wasn't supposed to make her so aware, so dependent on him—not here! But his touch sent her defenses tumbling, so that it was all she could do to keep herself from begging to be kissed.

Abruptly, Cass stopped his gentle stroking and dropped his hand to his lap "Not here," he said.

"Not here," she agreed.

"Can you do what I want you to do with 'Top Kid'?"

Peyton took refuge in Cass's retreat to business. "With your help." She paused, swallowed hard. "Cass, I'm sorry. I didn't mean to shut you out. I guess I've still got a lot to learn about being a program director."

"Not so much," he said quietly.

Cass watched her leave his office with a twinge of regret. Peyton was unlike every woman he'd known since Kate. No matter where he turned, what he did, he couldn't seem to leave her behind. And that disturbed him.

His life had been so neatly compartmentalized in the time between Peyton and Katie. There had been work, work, and work to fill the empty hours.

They were so different, Katie and Peyton. Or maybe it was just he who was different. Katie had always been a quiet accompaniment to his private life. She'd never concerned herself with the day-to-day business of radio, instead choosing to rule their home with love and good humor. So he'd been able to keep a separate life at work.

But radio was Peyton's lifeblood, and because of that she infused herself into all aspects of Cass's life. She appeared at work, at home, at play. Even in his sleep, he couldn't dismiss her. She was becoming too integral. The dividing walls that had kept his life neatly boxed were crumbling. And he had no idea how to cope.

Honesty. That was the key. But how to love again— that was the difficult part. He'd learned to be secretive about his private life—to wall off the prison of pain and emptiness he first experienced five years ago. He shared nothing more than he had to.

Now he wanted to love Peyton, but he no longer knew how. The habits of mistrust and emotional sterility had become too ingrained. He'd asked Peyton to trust him, but he still couldn't trust her with all the truths of his life.

Well, he'd gotten into the habit. He could surely break it. It was just a question of time.

Peyton had little chance to worry about "Top Kid." Three days later, the National Association of Radio Executives Conference Committee came to Columbus to oversee the final details for their meeting. Peyton spent two days squiring the group about town, showing them the city, the convention facilities and the outings she'd planned for spouses and guests.

She also arranged tours of 'FKN and other stations, meeting other station managers and spending time in the studio. The committee was uniformly impressed, and Peyton experienced a newfound camaraderie with the group. They liked and respected her and her work, and they made her comfortable with every decision she'd made.

Cass, too, spent time with the group, many of them colleagues from his days in New York. He particularly looked forward to visiting with Roger Forester, his former general manager and business partner.

Roger was a contrast to Cass: heavy-set, balding, sporting an iron-gray beard. But like Cass, he could be gruff and blunt. They'd been friends for years.

"That PD of yours, Peyton Adair," said Roger, "she's done a terrific job planning this conference. I'm really impressed."

"She's good." Cass smiled, trying to hide his inordinate pride at the compliment.

"She *is* good," Roger repeated. "She's done outstanding work on this convention. Not to mention what I've heard—and seen—about her ability to manage a station team. And if she can work with an old battleship like you . . ." Roger took liberties that came with years of friendship.

"That's very flattering," Cass said dryly.

"How long has she been with 'FKN?"

"Almost four years."

"How long as PD?"

"Two."

"And since then, 'FKN's market share has risen." It was a statement, not a question.

Cass nodded. "I'd like to think that has something to do with my leadership, too."

"Probably does. But a good PD helps."

"You're not thinking of trying to lure her away, are you, Forester?"

"I might. Do you know if she's thought about coming to New York to work?"

Cass was stunned. He couldn't blame Roger, of

course. He was just doing what every station manager with a slot to fill would do: look for the best candidate. But Peyton? His Peyton?

What would she do if she got this offer? It was her next logical career step, the goal she'd worked for most of her adult life.

Be flip. Treat it as a joke. Cass laughed. "What kind of offer are you making? It'd have to be pretty good for her to leave. She's training with the best, you know."

"Assistant program director," Roger said seriously. "Now that may sound like a step down, but the salary's quite good." He named a figure, and even with the cost of living calculated in, it was an impressive raise.

"What would she be doing?"

"Managing our nationally syndicated and satellite programming. She'd have a staff of about twenty."

Cass's face betrayed none of the panic he felt. Peyton's very dream was falling into her lap! How would he convince her to stay when Roger made this offer?

"Why's the position open?"

"Our assistant PD is leaving to take a job in Los Angeles. And our PD's expecting and doesn't want to work full-time once the baby's born. So despite the title, there's a lot of mobility right now—for the right person. I think Peyton might be the one."

For once, Cass was at a loss for words. "I don't know what to say."

"Tell me one thing: is she ready for New York?"

He could tell Roger no, that Peyton still needed time in a smaller market. But it would really be time for him to convince her—and himself—that they could build a life together.

Cass dismissed the thought almost as soon as it formed. He wouldn't sabotage Peyton's chances. He'd seen the fire in her eyes, the desire that burned on her

face. For him—and for her career. Bitter as the prosp
of her leaving might be, it would be far more bitter i.
she didn't make the choice herself. He no longer
wanted to utterly control people's lives. That was why
he'd come home.

So he answered truthfully. "She's ready."

"Jon, the fellow who's leaving, would be willing to
sublet his apartment to whomever we bring aboard."

"Such enticements!" But, in fact, it would be
enticing.

"Look," Roger said, as if reading Cass's mind, "I
don't have to make this offer right now. Jon's not leaving till January. And I understand that she has responsibilities here that she can't duck out of overnight. But
she's good, and everything you've said just makes her
seem better and better. I want her on my team."

"Did it occur to you that I might not want to let her
go?"

"You'll find a replacement for her . . ." Roger
stopped to study his old pal, and a note of concern
crept into his bluff speech. "Is there something going
on between you two?"

Then Roger's face lit up with glee. "Of course, you
don't want to let her go! You've fallen in love with
her! After all these years, you've finally come back to
the land of the living!"

"Well, it's something," Cass admitted. "I'm not
sure it's love yet. I'm not sure it'll ever be that."

"It's about time. We worried so much about you
after Katie died." Roger paused. "Cass, you just say
the word and I won't make her this offer. I can find
what I need elsewhere. You might not."

Another tempting chance. This time the effort cost
him less, as if having made one decision not to interfer
paved the way for other altruistic choices.

"No, Rog. You've got to give her the chance. Just do me a favor and wait a while. Give me a little time to convince her that I'm at least as good a gamble as the Big Apple."

"You sure?"

Cass nodded.

"Tell you what. Lots of offers are bandied about at the convention. I'll talk to her then. That gives you a few weeks to prep her."

"Thanks."

"Now about that other offer I've been nagging you about. . . ."

When Cass had ushered Roger back up to his hotel room, he allowed himself a moment of blind panic. What would happen to him if he lost Peyton now?

He didn't dwell on the prospect of a long-distance romance. He knew himself too well to even credit that as a possibility.

What *was* he ready for? He shrank from the possibility of marriage. Marriage meant opening himself to the possibility of that tremendous pain he'd vowed never to endure again. It was out of the question.

Could he admit that he cared for her? In words? Words had always been his forte, except where emotions ran deep. If he could somehow answer the love in her eyes . . . Dear God, this was hard! The habit of closing himself off was such a part of him. But somehow he had to do something so spectacular, so incredible, that Peyton would have no reason to accept Roger's offer. Something that would tie them together, that would hint at permanence.

Suddenly he knew what he would offer her. It wasn't marriage, it wasn't a declaration of love, but it might 〔d〕o. And it would surely ease the ache in his gut that 〔ca〕me at the thought of losing her.

EIGHT

"Well, that's over with!" Peyton turned to Cass as they waved good-bye to the last of the Conference Committee members at the airport. "I, for one, feel like celebrating."

"You've worked hard. You deserve a break. What do you say to a late dinner, after the show tonight?"

"I think all I want to do at that hour is go to bed."

"Champagne?" Cass suggested. "Raspberries? Fresh bread?"

Peyton's eyes widened and she ran her tongue over her lips. "You sure know how to tempt a woman! Raspberries in November!"

"I know this cozy out-of-the-way place with a fireplace. And the service is impeccable."

"Oh, why not?" She cocked her head, a twinkle of merriment in her eyes. "Do you suppose the boss would get really upset if I didn't come in until three tomorrow?"

Cass grinned mischievously and shook his head.

Their celebratory mood continued the rest of the day,

117

and Peyton somehow knew that tonight's feast was only the prelude to something bigger.

That evening, as Cass concluded the interview with his final guest, Peyton slipped off to the station's ladies' room. Shivering slightly with anticipation, she pulled the hairpins from her hair and let the cool chignon cascade down her neck. This was no night for prim and proper hairstyles. She brushed the strands until they gleamed, thinking regretfully that she shouldn't have let her hairdresser trim the ends quite so short last time. She liked Cass's fingers playing in her hair. She smudged a bit of color into her cheeks and lips and buffed her nose with powder. Not too bad for ten at night, she thought.

Cass draped his arm around Peyton as he left the studio. They walked through the station halls, causing a buzz of speculation among the station workers as they watched Cass envelop Peyton in a walking hug.

"This is a change!" Peyton whispered.

"Let 'em talk," Cass said. Perhaps if he were a little less circumspect in his relationship with Peyton, she'd begin to feel right about staying.

Peyton wasn't at all surprised that Cass bypassed several of the cozy restaurants with fireplaces that she knew. When they pulled into the driveway of Cass's farmhouse, she smiled to herself. The tingle of anticipation fired from every neuron, sending delicious tremblings racing along every fiber of her body.

"Are you cold?" Cass asked as Peyton shivered once again. "Let's go in the den and I'll start a fire before I get dinner."

She looked around as Cass knelt in front of the fireplace. Something was different, but she wasn't sure what. The wallpaper was still peeling in the corners and the afghan still hung askew over the back of the sofa. Frost had etched a snowflake pattern on the windows. Then she glanced over at the bookcase. The silver picture frame with Katie's picture was gone.

When had he put that away? And why? Did it mean that Cass was ready for her, for her love? Was the waiting finally over? Suddenly her shivering grew uncontrollable.

"You're cold!" Cass said as the fire licked its way through the kindling and caught hold of the larger logs. "Sit here by the fire and I'll bring you something warm to drink."

In a matter of minutes he reappeared with a wooden tray. It was laden with wholesome treats: crocks of steaming chicken soup, slabs of snowy bread smeared with butter, a dish of raspberries and cream and two flutes of champagne. Peyton sniffed the aromas appreciatively as Cass wrapped her hands around the soup bowl.

"This should thaw me out," she said, the words almost sticking in her throat. The feel of Cass's hands on hers and the nearness of his body started her quivering anew. He excited and aroused her like no man before. Sternly she reminded herself that despite the appearances, he *had* said he wanted time. She should enjoy this moment for what it was, not read new meanings into Cass's actions.

As Peyton ate, the soup's heat radiated deep into her bones. When she was warm, she raised the champagne glass in a toast. "To success," she said.

"To success," Cass agreed, "in every endeavor."

They clinked glasses, the golden liquid gleaming in the firelight. Then Cass wound his arm around Peyton's. His hand brushed her face as he leaned forward to sip out of his goblet.

If he's not setting the stage for a seduction, I don't

know what he's doing, Peyton thought as she swallowed. The champagne was cool and effervescent. It tickled her throat, buzzed in her ears. The sparkling wine pooled in her stomach and radiated heat through her limbs.

As the seconds passed and Cass made no effort to disengage himself, the champagne began to make her giddy. Forward. Fiery. She took another sip, taking care that the back of her hand smoothed Cass's cheek. His skin was warm, flushed from the wine and the fire. The blue of his eyes was barely visible; his lids were half closed.

Cass licked his lips slowly, as if daring her to come closer and claim them with her own. Well, she was feeling reckless. Whether it was from the success of the week or the success of the evening, she was unsure. But nothing could go wrong tonight. Tonight was hers.

She drained her champagne and deftly set aside both flutes. She reached for his face, cradling it between her palms. She ran her forefinger along the sharp outline of his nose, then rested her finger on his lips.

Cass edged his tongue out and captured her fingertip. He sucked slowly, evenly, generating a new core of heat in Peyton. She slid her hand along the high plane of his cheek, down his neck to his shoulder. She marveled at his strength, his utter physical perfection. It was so easy to love him. If only . . .

She shoved the thought away. She would allow herself this expression of her feelings. Cass was ready for sex; that was clear. If he still wasn't ready for love, well, she'd take her chances. She couldn't wait any longer.

The fire crackled and sparks flew up the chimney, lighting the way to perdition—or salvation. Peyton felt the even pressure of Cass's mouth on her finger, caressing, stroking, and her hot core became liquid fire. She withdrew her finger and pressed her lips to his, urging him to respond. Her mouth was firm, demanding.

"Peyton, there's something I want to tell you—"

"Shh, darling. No talking now."

Her mouth silenced his protests, blotting her lips of the slick sheen of lip gloss. Then it was skin on skin. The ridges of her lips played upon his, alternately insistent and pliant. Peyton could feel Cass's response, reluctant at first, then growing with an intensity to match hers.

He shouldn't be doing this. He should have resisted Peyton until he'd told her about Roger. About her big chance. But he couldn't find the right words to tell her. And now she'd completely robbed him of his glib gift of gab. He was grateful.

He feathered kisses down her cheek, reveling in the softness of her skin and the faint hint of jasmine. Jasmine—in the winter! Like Peyton, it was an unexpected balm in the middle of the relentless cold of existence.

He inched one hand up her shoulder, seeking the softness beneath her silk fisherman's pullover. With subtle skill, he eased the buttons loose at the neck, then slipped his fingers down to the velvet smoothness of her neck and shoulders. Slowly he outlined the bones that held Peyton together. He traced delicate designs in her flesh with his index finger, dipping and rising with each heaving breath she took.

He spread kisses over her face until he reached her ear. His hot breath enveloped it, sending paradoxical chills down Peyton's spine. Gently he tugged and nibbled until Peyton could stand no more and twisted away to exact sweet retribution.

She wound her arms around his neck, sliding her hands into his clean fresh hair. She pulled him down to her, gently lowering them both to the plush pile of the carpet. Hungrily, she answered his kisses, tasting and probing the contours of his mouth until she'd memorized each curve. She brushed her hand along the edge of his face, scratching her palm on the sandpaper of his beard, then following the line of his nose to his full eyebrows. She gently ruffled each one before running her hand back through the thick liquid silver of his head.

Then, as if learning his body by rote, she brought her hands forward across his neck. She buried her fingertips in the plush forest of hair that sprang from the throat of his flannel shirt as Cass sought her mouth again. She clumsily unbuttoned his shirt with one hand as the other followed, feeling the indentations of his skin along his ribs, testing the resilience of the muscle resting atop her.

"You feel so good," she murmured. "So strong."

Cass responded with a groan, low and febrile. He shifted his weight so that he lay askew, partly on the floor and partly on Peyton. Beneath the layers of clothing that separated them she could feel his desire pressed against her thigh. He propped himself on one elbow. Reverently he nudged her sweater up over her belly, her breasts, her neck, until he pulled it over her head and rolled it up as a pillow. He unfastened her bra, releasing Peyton's breasts to the glow of the fire.

Chest to chest, Cass's wiry carpet of hair caressed her tender flesh. Peyton shuddered with the sensation, wrapping her arms around Cass and pulling him tight. Cass sought her mouth again, this time fiery and eager, searing her with a passion beyond her experience. His tongue, demanding entrance to her mouth, was an incendiary mixture of hot and wet that plumbed the depths of each hidden crevice.

There was no escape. Cass had marked her as his, and Peyton knew with the joyful intuition of a woman in love that Cass adored her. He worshipped her body and he cherished her thoughts, holding each one dear. If he couldn't say so, his body spoke louder than any vocal protestations of love. He was hers, and there was no turning back. The waiting was over.

"Cass, oh, Cass," she moaned.

"I need you," he said in a throaty voice. "Dear God, I need you."

He bent down to claim her smoldering breast with his mouth, sucking her nipple to a blazing peak. Peyton gasped as her insides began to melt. Blindly she fumbled with the rivet that fastened his jeans, the straining zipper.

Released, Cass smoothly peeled away his remaining clothes. He lay against Peyton, hard and trim, and Peyton wrapped herself around him. She delighted in the sensation of his skin on hers, his buttocks tight and round in her hands. She ran her nails lightly across them, tickling him and making him writhe. He growled and pressed himself even more deeply against her.

"Undress me," she begged. "I want to feel all of you, with nothing between us."

He did. Slowly, carefully, Cass exposed Peyton's body to his. He picked her up and laid her on the floor by the fire, so that when he poised himself above her for the final act of love she would stay warm.

For what seemed like hours he caressed and teased, preparing Peyton for passion with the finesse of a master. He searched out the sensitive flesh of her inner thigh, kneaded the small of her back and stroked the baby-soft flesh of her abdomen, refusing Peyton's impatient pleas for satisfaction.

He made his actions a silent appeal to Peyton to

understand that he wanted her, needed her, desired her. If he couldn't tell her in words, he would do it with acts that unequivocally bespoke his feelings.

Peyton responded instinctively, with moans and pulsations of pleasure that defied her experience. Cass prodded and delighted her, finally reaching the triangle where Peyton kept her most secret self. With deft and skillful fingers, he soothed and caressed her, dipping into the river of moisture that declared she was ready, ready, more than ready.

He urged her on, rocking his hand against her intimately. She shivered, quaked with need, saving her final release to share with Cass.

She was never quite sure when Cass left her side to take up a position above her, but suddenly he was there, just as she thought she had no more stamina left, that she would die aching for Cass's fullness inside her. His manhood was luminous and strong. Leisurely he traced a pattern with its juices, between her breasts and over her abdomen until he rested lightly outside her pulsing inner coil.

Peyton could stand it no longer. He had teased her until she throbbed, until she could do nothing else but make him hers. Boldly she clasped his hard desire and guided its soft tip over her slick, secret folds.

"Not yet, Peyton," she heard him whisper in the mists of her mind.

But Peyton refused to wait. Arching her back, she rose to meet him. She guided him home, into the intimate depths of her femininity.

And Cass, once there, began the age-old dance of love. He pulled himself out and over her aching core, then drove back inside. Back and forth they moved together, conscious now only of an overwhelming need to surrender to the passion that consumed them with white-hot heat.

Peyton moved her body instinctively. It sang its own song now, a primeval melody of love and passion and fire. Intricate rhythms wove themselves as Cass withdrew and plundered, and her body resonated with descant harmonies. Higher and higher the pitch rose, and Peyton felt the melody's climax begin to rumble deep inside her.

And then she felt no more. Peyton's very essence imploded into Cass, and the wild white flames that had scorched them with desire burned back to embers.

They lay quiet for a time, breathing deeply. Peyton thought she had never felt anything richer and more satisfying than Cass, half beside her, half astride her. He'd buried his head on her shoulder, was using her silken hair as a pillow. Peyton smiled to herself.

"It was beautiful," she whispered.

"*You* are beautiful." He raised his head and looked at her, his face glistening with a thin film of dampness. Her whole body, bathed in the golden shadows of the firelight, glowed with contentment.

He had to tell her. Somehow he had to find the right words.

Tell her you love her. Tell her that, and the rest will follow.

But the words wouldn't come out. He could only look at her, strangled, mute. They were both trapped—by ambition, by the past, by everything but love. Love demanded too much.

Peyton saw the shadow that crossed his face. "Shh," she said, pulling his face to rest in the hollow of her neck to comfort him. "Don't worry. I knew what I was doing, and I wanted to. I've wanted to for a long time."

"Peyton, I have to tell you something."

"No words now," she chided gently, unwilling to hear that he regretted this beautiful evening. If he couldn't love her, so be it, but she wouldn't listen to it now. Now was for the afterglow of her own feelings, consummated with fire. She would deal with the rest of it tomorrow.

But tonight, tonight was theirs. Almost embarrassed at her own need, she stroked Cass's hair gently, fondled his smooth back and trim buttocks. She wanted him again, wanted to feel his weight atop her, wanted to revel in intimate kisses and sensual abandon.

Cass stirred as her fingertips roamed lazily over his sensitive skin.

"My God, woman, isn't once enough for you?" he teased.

"Oh, no. Not with you," she whispered. "Love me again, Cass."

This time was slow, even, hot coals burned back to ash. The fire mimicked their own passion, dying to glowing embers after hours of fiery heat.

Peyton was amazed at her response. Passion had never come so easily or made her so greedy.

"Another one," she wheedled as Cass raised his mouth to catch his breath. "Kiss me again."

"You have to promise to listen to what I have to say."

"No promises, Cass. I don't want promises. I want kisses."

He kissed her again, first her mouth, then her eyes, then along a trail down her shoulder to her breast. Peyton relaxed, warm with pleasure and secure in the knowledge that she could keep Cass interested. He wouldn't slay her feelings with cold hard truths tonight. The dawn would bring them soon enough.

NINE

When daybreak came, Peyton was nestled warmly in Cass's mahogany four-poster bed. Slowly she opened one eye and then the other to take in her surroundings.

Cass's bedroom was massive and masculine. The antique armoire and nightstand matched the bed. A sunshine yellow quilt was flung carelessly over a sturdy quilt rack, and a multicolored rag rug covered the hardwood floor next to the bed. The door to the adjoining master bath stood open. Peyton could see the antique motif carried on in the claw foot bathtub, pedestal washstand, and old-fashioned mosaic floor.

Only one thing was missing.

"Cass!" she called, then moaned at the sound of her voice breaking the morning stillness. Just her luck to fall in love with an early riser.

And she had fallen in love. It was pure, unadulterated love. Last night had just solidified and concentrated her feelings. In the cool gray of dawn, Peyton knew she'd found what she'd been wanting.

"Cass!" she called again. She willed herself to venture out of bed and rummage in the armoire for a bathrobe. *Only love could get me up this early when I don't have to*, she thought.

Then why, nagged a little voice, *couldn't Cass have stayed in bed for the same reason?*

Peyton wrapped herself in a navy terrycloth robe, rolled up the sleeves and knotted the belt snugly. She leaned against the wall and hugged her arms around her chest, recalling the ardor in his eyes, their smoky blue as he'd kissed and lapped and caressed her. He'd worshipped her body, desired her with a need as insatiable as her own. Together they'd soared to uncharted heights, then turned back towards earth to experience soul-wracking pleasure. She shuddered with the memory, a thrill skipping up her spine.

She breathed deeply and headed downstairs. She felt strangely heavy this morning, thick with love. She wanted Cass again, she realized, needed him to soothe her swollen limbs with sweetness and desire.

"Where are you?" she called again. Her voice echoed through the empty rooms. She looked out the front window, but Cass's jeep wasn't in the driveway. A wave of panic washed over her, but she quickly squelched it. Cass would have a logical explanation for his disappearance.

Of course he would, mocked that insidious voice. *It's perfectly normal for a man to leave the woman who's spent the night in his arms. It's a sure sign of love.*

Peyton put a kettle of water on the stove. The mundane act seemed to calm the storm brewing in her brain. She would not, as her father used to say, borrow trouble. Cass and she had to develop their own rhythm. They had obviously abandoned their decision to move slowly. But that just meant finding a new pace. They would learn about each other, trust each other, love each other. It was the only way.

And if Cass couldn't? What if he'd already run away, afraid of the intimacy, too fundamentally damaged ever to love again? The thought crept into her mind from her subconscious and once there, refused to budge.

As the kettle started to sing, she heard the crunch of tires against gravel. She ran to the window and peered out the curtains. Cass leapt down from the car. He carried a large paper sack.

"What are you doing awake, sleepyhead?" he asked as he closed the door behind him. The kettle whistled furiously. "I sneaked out to get goodies for breakfast in bed. Sounds like you're already at it."

Peyton heaved an involuntary sigh of relief. "I was worried when I woke up and you were gone. I didn't even remember going upstairs."

"I hope you didn't think I left you!" He voiced her wordless fear as he gathered her in his arms and held her close. Peyton relaxed, laying her warm cheek against the chill cotton of his jacket.

"We'd better get that teapot before it boils itself dry!" she said. "And I hope you brought plenty of food. I'm starved. I didn't eat much dinner, as I recall." She smiled.

"Bagels, donuts, croissants, milk, juice and eggs. I have coffee."

Breakfast was a decidedly decadent affair. Cass had sent Peyton back to bed with a cup of coffee, and he changed back into a bathrobe. When he reappeared in the doorway with warm plates of eggs and sweet rolls and frosted glasses of juice, she had almost fallen back asleep.

"Mm-mm!" Peyton ate slowly, savoring each bite. "You're quite a cook. I think I have to invite you over and show you that I'm no slouch in the kitchen, either.''

"You're no slouch anywhere." Cass grinned provocatively. "But if you're looking for an excuse—I'll bet you a home-cooked meal that Ohio State beats Michigan this weekend.''

"But Cass," she protested, "I wanted to fix *you* dinner. We're going to beat the pants off you Buckeyes!"

"Afraid to take the bet?"

"No way. But you're going to lose, big-time!"

"We'll see." Cass leaned over and kissed her. It was light and innocent, not at all the kind of kiss Peyton wanted. Her mind had planted too many doubts about the man beside her; she wanted to crowd them out with the hedonistic sensations only he could give.

"Move the dishes," she said in a husky tone. Then she snuggled closer and wiggled suggestively. "I think I'm ready for dessert."

"Dessert? At breakfast?" He drew apart the bathrobe and let his fingers play connect-the-dots with the tawny freckles on her chest. She closed her eyes and whimpered softly as Cass tugged open the belt and exposed the rest of her.

He smoothed his palm over her satiny skin, sinking into the hollow between her breasts and following the gentle contours of her belly to her thigh. His featherlight caresses grew bolder. He cupped one breast with his hand, kneading her nipple to berry hardness. He brought his mouth firmly over the other, sucking and nipping until it, too, stood tall.

"Love me," she begged.

"You're insatiable." Cass's voice was gravelly with desire as he slipped his fingers between Peyton's legs and nudged them wider. He rested his hand outside her throbbing core, drawing her heat from deep within.

Ever so slowly, Cass slid one finger across Peyton's warm center—stroking, stroking. He was delicate at first, dipping down to test her readiness for him. Then impatience took hold, and Cass intensified his pleasuring of her.

What had started as simple yearning grew into hunger, craving, and finally exquisite agony. Cass deepened his caresses, and Peyton raced for release. When it came, she rose up to meet him, spiraling toward freedom as waves of pleasure tore through her. She shuddered, moaned, and lay still.

Cass cupped his hand against her, catching the last ripples of release. They lay still for a few moments, smoldering with unreleased passion. Then Cass pulled Peyton atop him, sliding into the soft, dark depths of her femininity.

Peyton pushed herself upright, rubbing her hands across Cass's broad chest and twining her fingers into the luxuriant blond hair that covered him. She caressed him, running her hands lightly over his nipples, causing them to rise to rigid peaks. She brushed her hands along his sides; he shivered and squirmed.

"Stop that!" he rasped. "You're giving me goosebumps!"

"It's no more than you do to me," she whispered. But she stopped tickling and began to concentrate on more immediate needs. She moved slightly to position Cass more deeply within her and, with a rhythm as old as time, she rocked him home.

Cass's features became stony, then slack as he reached that private place where only lovers travel. Without a word, he reached the pinnacle of human release. Watching him, Peyton felt her passion pour over him, bathe him in emotion so pure she couldn't hide it.

"Cass, oh, Cass," she murmured. "I love you."

She knew the instant the words were out of her mouth that they were the wrong thing to say. The words "I love you" demanded a response. She and Cass had already rushed the decision about lovemaking; now she was forcing open declarations of that emotion. Her timing couldn't have been worse.

"What did you say?" Cass asked, opening his eyes.

He was giving her a chance to take it back and deny what she'd said.

She couldn't.

She opened her mouth to say, "Nothing," but the sounds wouldn't emerge from her throat. She had spoken the truth, and no matter what difficulties the truth brought, she could not refute it.

"I love you," she said helplessly.

"I don't suppose we could forget you said that?"

She shook her head mutely.

Cass pulled her down so that her breasts flattened against his chest. He wrapped his arms around her to stave off the chill morning air. "Peyton, dear Peyton. I wish I had the answer you want."

"I'm not asking for one. I know my timing's awful. But I can't help how I feel. I couldn't share . . . this . . . without love."

"Don't you deserve better than me? Someone more predictable, more reliable? You're a wonderful woman, Peyton. Warm and trusting and open. I don't know if I can be what you need. What you deserve."

Peyton saw the pain in Cass's face as he spoke, and she tried to reassure him. "You're what I want. The more I see of you, the more I want you. But we won't work if you keep clinging to what you've been, if you're afraid to let yourself feel love again."

"I've forgotten how."

"I don't believe that. You're warm and funny. You're a terrific radio host. You know what you're doing and why. And you want to change. Or that's what you told me."

"I thought I could do it myself, gradually. I wasn't counting on you."

"Isn't that what makes life grand? The unexpected pleasures?" She grew serious again. "Cass, I can't help the way I feel. You're worth having. I'm willing to wait—and work—for you. However long it takes. But only if—"

"If what?"

She fumbled for the right words. There was so much she wanted to say, about love, trust, patience, and hope. She'd been terribly greedy this morning. She'd offered Cass implicit faith, expecting him to return the favor. She'd forgotten the basic tenet of love: selflessness. Cass had to find his own answers, his own definition of love. All she could do was love him.

And hope that he found his answer in her.

"We can't look to the past for answers. We have to trust each other. I know love can't be forced. We have to take our time—and the answer will come. One way or another."

"How did you get so smart so young? It's taken me thirty-eight years to slow down enough to learn things like that. Even now I'm not sure I really know them."

"My family taught me a lot about love and patience and working for what you want. And about when not to back down." Peyton ran her hand down Cass's chest, twirling her fingers in the lush carpet of hair that covered him. "I don't want to back down with you."

Cass lay silent for a long while, aimlessly stroking Peyton's hair. "I don't have your courage, Peyton. Take care of yourself. I don't want to hurt you."

* * *

"I told you to let me drive. I have a campus parking permit. We wouldn't be stuck in this traffic jam if you'd listened."

Cass shifted the Jeep into second gear and swore softly as a bright red Camaro cut him off. "You're just mad because Michigan lost the football game—and you have to fix supper."

"We were robbed! Robinson should've been called for holding. Instead they gave you a first down. And a lucky field goal. Kane never should've made it from fifty yards out."

"Any way you look at it, the scoreboard said 24–21, OSU. And you're cooking."

Peyton grinned sheepishly. "We have to stop at the grocery. I was a little too sure of myself, and I didn't buy anything for dinner."

"I'm crushed. Here I thought I was going to be pampered, and you're telling me I have to go shopping."

"I presume *you* had everything in your fridge, just in case."

"Absolutely. Cornish hens, wild rice, broccoli and hollandaise sauce, and lemon chiffon pie." He pulled out into the traffic and accelerated smoothly. "So, which grocery are we going to hit? Or should we just call out for pizza?"

"This was supposed to be my chance to show you I can cook, remember? We're not eating pizza!" She glared in mock annoyance, then broke into ringing laughter.

The day had been such fun, despite the November cold. They'd started with an indoor tailgate party at the station, then moved on to the stadium for a few crazy minutes playing "how many people can we fit in the broadcast booth." Once in their seats, they'd kept warm by cheering on their respective teams as the score seesawed back and forth.

Most important, she and Cass were talking and joking like normal people who didn't suffer from unrequited love. All in all, it had been a very fine day.

Oh, Cass was still afraid. She knew that. He was afraid of his past, afraid of caring again. She'd seen it in his eyes and heard it in his voice when he'd told her to be careful.

She'd seen it off and on during the past week. A humorous remark or gesture would catch him off guard, and he'd react with an odd glance or dispirited shrug of the shoulders. She'd even seen it once or twice today, when he thought she wasn't watching, a brief lapse into pensiveness, a far-away wistful stare.

But his fears didn't overshadow everything they did. They had relaxed and eased the tension caused by her premature admission of love. They were laughing, hoping, caring.

And most important, she'd convinced herself that she could wait for him—as long as she needed to, because Cass was worth it. Worth waiting and hoping and dreaming for. One night in his arms had persuaded her of that.

And the day wasn't over yet. There was the promise of dinner, wine, and an encore performance of Cass's fireside magic.

"The shopping won't take long," she assured Cass as he wheeled into the parking lot. "You stay put. Dinner's going to be a surprise."

Twenty minutes later Cass was seated in Peyton's living room, opening the white wine. He poured two glasses and brought one to Peyton in the kitchen.

"Go, Bucks!" he teased, raising his glass.

"To whatever makes you happy," she agreed.

The wine was cool and fruity, with just enough tang to make a second glass inevitable. Peyton hummed as she chopped vegetables, boiled pasta, and stirred sauces. The night was still young.

She set the table for two, using ivory candles and bright, whimsical stoneware. Thick, handwoven napkins rested on the plates.

"Dinner's ready," she called.

"Everything's lovely," Cass said as he sat down. He poured Peyton another glass of wine and emptied the last drops from the bottle into his glass.

"There's an old French saying that whoever drinks the last drop from a bottle of wine will soon be in love," Peyton teased.

He peered at the vintner's label. "I'm sure that's only true of French wine. This one's from California. I'm safe!"

"Cass, Cass, where's your sense of romance?"

"Right here." He reached over and pulled a mum from the centerpiece. Deftly he shortened the stem and tucked the flower between her breasts. He leaned over to catch the subtle scent and brushed his finger lightly across the skin of her throat. Down, down he moved until he caressed the petals of the blossom, and Peyton quivered, imagining it was her flesh beneath his hand. She scarcely dared breathe; the moment seemed so close, so intimate.

Slowly, almost reluctantly, Cass withdrew. They watched each other for a minute, gathering their thoughts and their emotions.

Cass broke the stillness with a lighthearted question. "So what do you want to do when you grow up?"

Suddenly Peyton was ready to share her soul. Cass had a right to know her dreams. After all, she wanted him as part of them. And if she could share herself, surely he would follow. She would talk of the future, the future they'd been so assiduously avoiding.

Flush with wine and drunk with love, Peyton answered candidly. "I want to work in New York some day."

"That's a tough market."

"I don't want to stay there forever. Just long enough to learn what I need to know so I can own my own station."

"Big dreams."

"It doesn't have to be a big station. Not even as big as 'FKN. Just a place where I can help kids get started in this business, like my first GM helped me."

"Where do you want your station?"

"Somewhere not too far from Detroit. That's one of the things I love about Columbus. It's far enough away from home—and close enough. I'll miss that when I'm in New York."

"When is all this going to happen?"

"Oh, heck, I don't know. When it's right. Next year, two years. I don't have a timetable. Besides, there are other things that are just as important as my career in radio."

"Oh?"

"I love teaching. Someday I'd like to be more than an adjunct instructor. Can't you see me as an academic, writing long papers on the sociological implications of shock radio?"

"No." He laughed. "How could any student respect a professor whose office is in the shape yours always is?"

"At least *I* always know where my tapes are! Which is more than we can say for you."

"Don't bait the boss. He has a tough time keeping the whole station straight."

"But do you know what I really want, most of all?"

Her eyes grew soft and dewy, and she leaned forward. The flower tumbled out of her blouse.

"A pink Cadillac?"

She shook her head solemnly. "Love. I want to get married and have a family. It was always a vague and distant dream. I don't think I *really* wanted it until now. Until you."

The words hung in the air like stifling humidity. Now she'd done it. For all her fine words about waiting patiently, she'd gone and brought up love and their future. Again. Why was it that suddenly everything—all her hopes and dreams—seemed centered on the personal? On Cass?

This isn't right, she told herself firmly. *It's not fair to pin my future on Cass. Not to him and not to me. I have dreams and ambitions, and I have to be ready to take them up if Cass can't love me back. Which he never will if I don't back off.*

"I know it's too soon to think about this, Cass. Every time we talk about something important, I seem to get two steps ahead of the game. I'm sorry. I know you can't talk about it yet. And I'm willing to wait." She paused, studying Cass for a reaction. Gone was the glint of good humor, the companionable ribbing. All she could detect was a cold sadness.

Well, what had she expected? What did she really know about what he wanted? He'd said he wanted a chance to return to his roots, a chance to find some peace. But her? Marriage? There were no guarantees. Especially not with a man who'd locked his heart away.

She said softly, "What about you? What do you want?"

"Peyton, don't hope for too much. There's so much you don't know . . ."

"Can't you tell me?" she pleaded. "I can help."

"Peyton, don't you understand that there are things I can't discuss? Things too personal, too private. Things I'm not ready to talk about because I don't know what I believe about them yet. I have to work out my problems myself."

"But it's so lonely that way!" Peyton protested. "I'm willing to listen."

"But I'm not looking for an ear. Don't push, Peyton." His voice, though soft, held an undertone of steel, and his eyes were dark. "It won't work."

Peyton sighed. They were quarreling, and it was all her fault. She knew Cass was a very private person. Yet every chance she had, she baited him, trying to force admissions he couldn't feel yet. *I'm not desperate*, she thought. *So why am I acting like a fool?*

"I'm sorry." But the mood she'd been trying to create over supper was broken. She needed a few minutes to regroup, to get her mind back to the lighthearted moments of this afternoon. "Why don't you call the station and get our messages while I finish dessert? You can use the phone in my room."

"Good idea." Cass walked down the short hall and closed her door firmly behind him.

Damn! Her common sense had abandoned her. All she could do was put her foot in her mouth. *Maybe I'm not as patient as I thought I could be*, she thought bitterly. *In my own way, I'm just as demanding, just as tough as Cass. I can't just let things be.*

Peyton busied herself with the dishes, but she couldn't dismiss the unpleasant comparisons she'd made between her and Cass. They had no future if she didn't develop some patience—fast.

The minutes ticked by, and still Cass hadn't emerged from her room. Either something is really wrong at work, she thought as she rinsed the last of the dishes, or Cass is having the same kind of second thoughts that are plaguing me.

She was setting the dessert dishes on the table when Cass reappeared. His step was deliberate and his face impassive. He still seemed distant and removed. Peyton's heart sank to her toes. The evening was on a headlong course to failure.

"Everything okay at work?" she asked.

"That depends on whether you wanted to leave town for Thanksgiving."

"I hadn't planned to. What's up?"

"I have to attend to some unfinished business in New York. If I go, that leaves you in charge."

"That's no problem. What's in New York?"

"Just some . . . papers I need to sign." He coughed. "Property . . . transactions."

They ate their dessert quietly, but curiosity gnawed at Peyton. This trip was so sudden, too convenient. Just as they were beginning to carve out a space for themselves, as rocky and unfinished as the place might be, Cass had to leave for New York. He was going back to the source of his fears and distractions. It did not bode well.

"Can't your attorney handle it?" she asked gently. "It would be nice to have you around for Thanksgiving."

"I need to go, Peyton." He looked at her, unflinching. "Let me go."

He's backing away, she realized sadly. *Because I've done nothing but push. He needs me to accept him for what he is, and I can only see him for what he can be. I'm always looking for something more.*

The silence grew longer and longer. They cleared the table and washed the last of the dishes, carefully avoiding touching one another. Cass's skin radiated heat, and Peyton couldn't bear the burning sensation that only a few days ago she'd basked in. It was too painful. She was losing the game, the match, the set.

Damn and damn again! What was it about Cass that drove her so hard and fast, that made her take such dangerous chances?

She'd always been a team player, ready to make sacrifices for the benefit of all. But with Cass, all those years of training flew right out the window. She *knew* he wasn't ready, that she shouldn't push too quickly. But some part of her, the part connected to her mouth, kept ignoring reality, kept on pushing, like a runner bound on winning the Boston Marathon.

"It's been a long day," he said finally. "I think I could use some sleep."

"Yeah," she said a trifle too fast.

"I'm leaving tomorrow morning. Here's the number where you can reach me if you need to." He handed her a scrap of paper scrawled with digits, but his fingers didn't brush against hers. "I should be back on Sunday. Use your own judgment about which tapes to use for 'On Air Columbus' and do what you can about rescheduling the week's guests."

"Fine." She put more enthusiasm in her voice than she felt. "Don't worry about things here. We'll manage."

"Goodnight, Peyton. Thanks for dinner. You really can cook." A shadow of a smile curved his lips, then faded. He picked up his belongings, opened the door and walked to the Jeep.

There would be no repeat performance of their fiery need for each other, no chance to redeem in action and passion the hasty words she'd delivered over dinner. He hadn't offered her so much as a kiss good-bye.

Peyton leaned against the doorjamb and wrapped her

arms around her middle, trying to keep the sick feeling in her stomach at bay. This morning she'd had such hope. Now it was all she could do to plan for tomorrow.

Cass was leaving. For now, and maybe for good. And without him, nothing tied her to Columbus.

Oh, he'd be back. His life was here. But there were no guarantees that he'd want her with him.

The night air was cold, but Peyton was so thoroughly chilled by the moment that it made little difference. She watched Cass's taillights dwindle to tiny points of red.

She could have cried. Everything that had so suddenly and sharply come into focus the last week was blurring and slipping away. She'd become demanding, razor sharp. Cass could only retreat, frightened by the whole prospect of love and surrender. And she was only making it more difficult to wave the white flag. Her terms were too intense.

"Cass," she moaned. "I'm sorry. I want to help, but I only seem to make it worse. I'm too impatient and you're too scared." Her last words were whispered. "I don't think we can ever work."

A lone tear slid down her cheek, and she wept for what might-have-been, for his fears, for hers, for their failure.

She had to take care of herself. Cass had said that. She'd let herself get sidetracked by starry-eyed visions of happily ever after, visions that he couldn't share. Visions that she'd tried to force.

It was time to face reality. She might want Cass in her future, but if it weren't mutual, it would never work. It wasn't working now.

She had to keep herself at a distance, far enough away so that Cass could come to her if he wanted, far enough away that he didn't feel he had to. She would talk with him when he got back. She would make a few discreet inquiries at the convention.

Maybe it was time to stretch her wings.

TEN

The flight to New York was hell. Turbulence and thunderstorms only heightened Cass's already irritable state. Dire warning from his accountants and attorneys rang in his ears.

"Potentially serious cash flow problems."

"Payroll. Benefits. Payables."

"We strongly recommend against concluding this deal now."

And the memories . . . Katie, bright and golden as the sun on their wedding day, dancing on the waves in Hawaii, planting petunias every spring . . . lying cold and still in a satin-lined box . . .

Well, what did he expect? He *was* going to New York to testify at a parole hearing. Why wouldn't the prospect of facing Katie's killers dredge up memories?

Those two crackheads had completely changed his life: stolen his wife and blasted his sense of compassion to bits. He could never forgive them, and by God, neither would the State of New York.

He shifted in his seat, gazed out across the wing of

the jumbo jet. The clouds surrounding the plane were gray and threatening; they matched Cass's mood well.

It was all so unfair—what those boys had done to themselves, to him, to Katie.

What he was doing even now to Peyton.

Cass wrapped his hands around the plastic cup on the tray before him, his third. The cold of the ice penetrated his fingertips. Lifting the glass, he rattled it, swirling the amber liquid over the cubes. Then he drained it with a quick jerk of his head.

The liquor burned all the way down, filling the hollowness of his gut with false heat, false courage—the kind he needed in order to face the days ahead. He had none of the real stuff left.

If he had any real courage, he'd accept what was due him: a dull ache, a faded grief, and justice, not forgiveness. He'd stop thinking about Peyton, about Katie. He'd stop wishing for things that were no longer within his grasp, things he no longer had any right to ask for, things like peace and solace.

Instead, he got memories—full force. And he got Peyton, her skin glowing in the firelight, her body warm and pliant from loving. And he was unable to share his soul with her, capable only of running away.

He signaled the flight attendant for another Scotch.

Face it, Sloane. You've got nothing left to give her. You're tied to the past, tied to too many secrets. You couldn't even tell her what this trip was all about. You never told her how your marriage really ended.

"Peyton!" Sally stuck her head in Peyton's office door and bounded in without waiting for an invitation. "You'll never guess what just happened!"

From the tone of Sally's voice, Peyton decided she'd brought good news. She smiled weakly, wishing she could muster more enthusiasm. But the past few days had been a trial, coping without Cass, realizing that all her fears of a future without him might truly come to pass.

Not that she couldn't go on without him. Survival wasn't the issue. But everything that made life more than survival had withered. The joy of living had departed that evening with Cass.

But the white-hot knife of desire still tormented her at night. Memories and dreams flooded her and mingled until she couldn't tell which were which. Had she really lain in his arms, on the edge of forever? Or was this ache of wanting nothing more than a terrible chimera, a parody of genuine emotion? Was the insatiable pull of release, spreading through every pore of her body like lava, no more than a romantic fantasy?

Daylight carried its own pain. Here she replayed all their encounters without the benefit of sleep to soften the edges. Everything grew bigger, loomed more ominously. Here she faced the reality that Cass, whom she'd loved like no other, could not love her. In daylight she had to accept that he was still running.

Only work—the fact that thousands of people counted on the station to keep them informed and entertained—provided any distraction from the memories and hopes that battered her.

"I hope you're not bringing me any problems," Peyton warned Sally playfully, though her heart wasn't in the teasing.

"FCC investigation?" Sally responded in kind. Then, seeing the startled look Peyton shot her, she added hastily, "Just kidding."

Sally perched on the edge of Peyton's desk. "This is great news."

"So 'fess up." Peyton pushed away the pile of papers in front of her and focused her attention on her friend.

Sally took a deep breath, made a dramatic sweep of her hand and said, "I quit."

Peyton was prepared for any number of announcements but this declaration came as a stunning blow. She stared at Sally in disbelief, eyes wide and mouth trembling.

Some days you just couldn't count on anything.

"What?" she asked, though she'd understood Sally's words perfectly well. "Why? What's going on? I need you till this conference's over."

"Hold on, honey," Sally reassured her, grabbing her hands and squeezing tight. "I didn't mean to scare you."

"Well, you did. What's this nonsense about your quitting? I thought you wanted some experience."

"I did. And believe it or not, it's already paid off."

"What are you saying?" At the look of glee on Sally's face, Peyton divined the answer. "You found a job!"

"Not just a job—a future."

Peyton's spirits lifted at Sally's good news. At least one of them was doing better. The bout of unemployment had left Sally drained, depressed, and doubtful, alternately sure that her big break was right around the corner or positive that she would never work ever again. Thank goodness someone had recognized what Peyton already knew—that Sally Ashton was a treasure.

"Where? When? Talk to me, Sal!"

"Just north of here—a little rural station. I'll mostly be handling the programming, but there's room for me in sales, too. And if we're all happy with each other at the end of my contract, there's a chance to buy into the business."

"I'm so glad for you. It sounds great. But when are you leaving?"

"Now don't panic. I told them I couldn't start until the first of the year, and it's cool." Sally chuckled. "Can you imagine! They think I'm worth waiting for! In fact, I beat out several younger people for the job. They said they liked my maturity and level head."

"Gray hair and all, huh?" Peyton vamped.

"Well, my age is a liability in this business. That and my lack of management experience. But you gave me a chance—and a lot of confidence—when I was down. I owe you, Peyton."

Peyton shook her head. "I'm just glad it finally worked out. When Cass fired you and everybody else, I was ready to walk, too."

"I've learned. Never leave a job without another firmly in hand," Sally said sagely.

Peyton shook her head again. "Sometimes I wish I had, Sal. Things would've been much easier."

"What's the matter?"

Peyton looked at Sally mournfully. "Cass . . . me . . . us."

Sally glared at her expectantly, so Peyton continued, "He's gone, you know. Off to New York."

"Why?"

"A property deal, he said, but I don't think that's the real reason."

"What is?"

"I've scared him off. Too much talk of love and marriage and children."

"What's wrong with that?" Sally demanded. "I've spent a good part of my life doing just those things!"

"Yeah, but you're not Cass." Peyton sighed and leaned back, lifting her hair off her neck and letting it drop around her shoulders. "I keep crowding him, so he closes himself off. I can't help if he won't let me in.''

Sally whistled softly. "This doesn't sound good, kid. Five years is a long time. Long enough to develop some really bad habits."

"I thought we were getting somewhere. We were happy together, we did silly things, and then . . . It all changed after that last committee meeting. He was so affectionate that night, he even put his arm around me here at the station. And then we went to his house, he fixed some dinner . . ."

"And breakfast?" Sally prompted.

Peyton nodded, coloring faintly at the recollection. "It was wonderful. He was wonderful. But I couldn't let it be enough. I wanted more—promises, a future, declarations of love . . ."

"There's nothing wrong with wanting that. Society, life itself, are built on those things."

"But I didn't need them that very minute," she whispered. "That's the point. I'm moving too fast. Cass can't keep up."

Sally pursed her lips in thought. Finally she said, "Something's missing from this puzzle. A man who's had a good marriage, even one that ended as tragically as Cass's did, shouldn't be so terrified of a relationship."

"What do you mean?"

"Something else is going on." At Peyton's incredulous look, Sally said slowly, "If Jack died tomorrow, God forbid, I'd be heartbroken. But we've had thirty good years, and we've been happy. So if I ever found another man who loved me even half as much as Jack, I'd marry him in a second. Because a good marriage is the best way to live."

"So you think Cass and Katie weren't . . ."

Sally shrugged. "It might explain a lot."

"I don't know, Sal. I believed him when he told me about Katie. The pain was real."

"Sure it was. But the fear is out of place."

"So what do I do?" Peyton said woefully, pushing her hair from her forehead. "How can I control myself? How can I make him believe in me?"

Sally took her time answering, as if considering her words carefully. And Peyton knew with certainty that she had no ordinary problem, for Sally rarely came up short for conversation. "Maybe you can't," she said finally.

"You mean it's hopeless."

"Oh, honey, I wish I had some decent advice. If I didn't have Jack and the kids, who knows where I'd be. And if you can build that with Cass, so much the better. But I also know that you can only do so much to make him trust you. After that, he has to reciprocate."

"If he doesn't?"

"Then you've got to cut loose." Sally reached over and put her hand on Peyton's shoulder, looked her full square in the eyes. "And that's when it hurts the most."

"Petition for parole will be taken under advisement. The board will notify the interested parties of its decision."

Cass rose stiffly and turned to leave, his carriage tight and restrained. He desperately needed to get outside, away from the close confines of the tiny room. He was ready to explode.

The hearing had been simple: the prosecutor arguing against parole; the tired public defender pointing out that the two men had been in drug rehab for years and were ready for a second chance in society. The two men crying that they were sorry, that they had paid for their crime.

Cass's own words were full of pain, anger, and impotence. He hadn't been able to breathe; every fiber of his body had screamed with memories. Of himself, of Katie, of everything he no longer was and could no longer be. And why? Because these boys—men now—had jerked Katie out of life, leaving him to face the truth about himself alone.

And the truth was that he'd actually lost Katie twice: once to the finality of death . . . and just before that, even more shattering, through his own stupidity. He knew that now, too late, of course, to make amends.

Cass stepped outside the old stone building. The day was bright, unseasonably clear, and the light hurt his eyes. He blinked rapidly, holding back the automatic moisture that rushed to protect him from the sun's brilliance.

He still had to see Roger Forester today, finish that deal and work out the details of another one long in the works. If he kept busy, rushing here and there, he could douse the flames of recall that licked the edges of consciousness—and conscience.

But that would only last until the night, when business couldn't occupy any more time or energy. Then it would all come to him, the truth he'd tried to bury with Katie, the real reason he couldn't give Peyton what she merited, the real scars hidden below the obvious ones.

He hailed a cab and told the driver to head uptown. He'd concluded his deals first. Always business first. It was the only way he knew to survive.

But when the deals were finished and the ink on the signatures dry, Cass went back to the hotel. He'd refused Roger's offer of dinner, declined a party invitation, foregone the celebratory champagne toasts. He wanted and needed to be alone—insisted on it, so he could bob and churn in a whirlpool of self-reproach.

What had happened to him? How had he driven Katie away?

At first their life had been easy. They'd moved around the country so often that life was an adventure. They explored their new home by day; Cass worked by night. They lived an inside-out existence, their schedules out of sync with potential friends. In those early years all they had—all they needed—was each other.

But somehow that changed. The longed-for chance at New York arrived, a seat in the middle of excitement and glory. New York was Cass's opportunity for national success, the kind that brings money and power. And he'd changed.

Perhaps there was no single trigger. But his arrogance, his pride, his engulfing ambition blinded him to Katie's needs. He grew obsessed with work, with ratings and influence, with trends and self-importance. He climbed popularity charts and tax brackets, and somehow, somewhere, he left Katie behind.

Ironically, he didn't realize it. Not then, anyhow. After all, Katie was still with him—in the most concrete sense. She lived under the same roof, shared his bed, took his shirts to the cleaners, and fixed his meals when he was home. She was always there.

But he'd abandoned her just as surely as if he'd walked out on her. Late nights, power meetings, schemes and deals effectively locked Katie out of his life.

Katie tried to point that out occasionally, calmly, telling him she'd had enough of the bright lights. She wanted to go back home and start raising their family. She wanted their old life back. She wanted the man she'd married, not the spoiled celebrity he'd become.

He hadn't listened when she started making threats, either. They were quiet, in Katie's usual way. He had a year . . . six months . . . two weeks. The deadlines sped by, but Cass never took them seriously. He thought she was teasing, that he had plenty of time. He always had time. Just as he always had Katie.

Until that night he came home, late as usual, to find two suitcases standing in the foyer of their elegant east side co-op. He was confused; Katie sometimes visited her parents without him, but she always gave him plenty of notice.

The apartment was dark, and as he flicked on lights, he saw that things were missing: a small print from the wall—Katie's favorite; a lacquered box they'd found in Chinatown; the porcelain figurine that had decorated their wedding cake.

Cass's heart began to beat faster, and he crossed the living room swiftly. What was going on? Where was she? What had happened to his wife?

She wasn't in their room, nor in the study where she sometimes waited up for him. She wasn't in the kitchen, not in the bathroom, and not on the balcony where she liked to watch the city lights twinkle and blink.

Cass's heart snagged in his throat when he discovered her sleeping in the guest room. The adrenaline washed out of him. Emptiness replaced panic. It was more potent, more terrifying than fear.

Katie had pulled the bedclothes fiercely around her and curled her body into a tight ball. There was a defensiveness about her he'd never seen before, and she'd been crying. The light from the hall shone on the uneven red patches near her eyes.

"Kate," he said softly, sitting on the side of the bed. "Katie, hon, what's wrong? Are you sick?"

She awoke with a start, as if she'd never meant to sleep. She edged down and out of the bed and slipped into her robe, an old flannel number she'd bought when they lived in Minnesota. She cinched the belt around her sharply. "I'm leaving," she said simply.

"What?" Her statement laid him low, like a right hook to the stomach. He couldn't believe his ears. His wife? Leaving? She couldn't. She was the only constant in his life. He . . . needed her. Didn't she know that?

"I'm leaving," she repeated stoically. "Your year is up. I'm going home."

"But why? What's wrong?" His mind flew to the only reason he could conceive of. "Is there someone else?"

She shook her head.

"Then what?" Pain, quick and sharp, tore at his voice. *"Why?"*

Katie folded her arms around her middle protectively and backed into the hallway, the light harsh on her pale, golden features.

Her voice came through to him now, sad and breaking. "This life is killing me . . . killing us. I don't know you any more. You come home at all hours, leave before dawn. . . . You're different now, and I want the man I married, the one I love, the one who loved me . . ."

I do love you! But the words caught in his chest, the truth of her grief slamming home.

Her voice trembled and she hugged herself harder. "I want a family, a real home, a husband—and I can't have that with you the way you are now."

"Katie," he muttered, still in shock. "We've been married thirteen years. Doesn't that count?"

"If you'd listen to me. But you moved away a long time ago. And now I've got to move, too."

"But it's so sudden!"

No sooner were the words out of his mouth than he remembered the deadlines he'd ignored, the quiet determination of her only demand in thirteen years. He'd been supremely confident that she was joking.

And now he would pay for that arrogant mistake.

"Do you really want this, Kate?" he whispered. "Do you want out?"

Tears glistened in her eyes, and Cass felt the sting of his own. He'd taken her for granted, cut her out of his life. And now she was cutting him out of hers.

He held his breath, waiting for her answer. He could feel his heart thud against his ribs, waves of nausea rushing through him. He'd never felt so threatened, so terrified.

"I want *you* back," she said finally. "You, before 'success' turned you into whatever you are now." She tilted her head up at him, as if daring him to deny he'd changed so drastically.

"How?" he said desperately, ready to agree to anything, anything to rid himself of the awful prospect that Katie might leave.

"Counseling."

His sense of privacy rebelled. "A stranger?"

"Someone objective," she corrected him. "Someone who can see if there's anything left worth saving. It's the only way I'll stay."

Trapped, defeated, wounded beyond healing, Cass had agreed. The next day, she was dead, cornered by a gang of teenagers crashing on cocaine and desperate for enough money for another hit.

She'd been on her way to their first session with the marriage counselor.

The role of grieving widower came easily. No one ever suspected that Fate had just substituted one brutal ending for another. Work drove him, compelled him, kept him from thinking about the truth—that Katie had given up on him.

And finally, when the rage became too much, when he finally recognized what Katie had tried to make him see, he abandoned that life.

But it was too late.

Even five years later, the first image he summoned when he thought of Katie was how she'd been that night: hunched in, fragile, breaking his heart as he'd broken hers. He would not risk that again, wouldn't risk hurting Peyton the way he'd hurt Katie.

But he'd been damn close to trying. Thank God for the hearing, for the deal with Roger, for the million other details he had to attend to here. Coming back to New York had given him the perspective he lost when he was with Peyton. With her around, he could almost believe again: that he and Katie could have made it, that he and Peyton would.

He'd never told anyone that his marriage had been collapsing around him, another casualty to the stresses of the media lifestyle. But *he* knew. And in the quiet, sterile hotel he acknowledged both the joy of a good marriage and the inevitable pain that came with drifting apart—the inevitable loss that came from loving him.

In Columbus, he'd tried to forget that truth. But here, in the cold reality of New York, in the city he'd shared with the woman he both loved and destroyed, he couldn't help but remember. He could never be what Peyton needed, what she deserved. He was scarred, bitter, cruel perhaps. He lied, even to himself.

He had broken Katie and ruined himself. And he would do it again, this time to Peyton, if he were stupid enough to try.

He was a coward. He couldn't go forward and he

couldn't go back. He was stuck in a hell of his own fashioning, caged by memory, shackled by pain. Everywhere he turned, truth and justice mocked him.

He'd nearly convinced himself that maybe he and Peyton could work, given enough time. That they could build a life based on affection and their shared passion for radio. No skyrockets, no dizzying heights, but a solid bond of companionship. It might have been enough—until she'd shared her wide-eyed hopes and dreams: New York, marriage, family.

It had brought him face to face with his own dreams. A lot of people wouldn't call them dreams at all, but they were all Cass could bear. He no longer wanted the rollercoaster highs and lows, the soul-baring, gut-wrenching joy and sorrow of real love.

And loving Peyton would require all that. And more.

He didn't want a family; Katie had offered that once and he'd refused. He didn't want New York; it had robbed him of everything he'd ever valued. He didn't want. . . .

But he did. He wanted Peyton with every fragment of his shattered heart, with every bit of his lacerated life. But it could never be enough. He could never offer Peyton more than hints of the man he'd been, broken pieces of character, secrets hidden, and wry, bitter humor. Little hope. Low expectations.

Peyton didn't understand the compromise that staying with him demanded. And if she did, she would never be satisfied. They would come to an end as he and Katie had—troubled, wounded, aching.

He'd had enough of that kind of hurt, and he wouldn't subject Peyton to it. She deserved better.

The trip had been hell. But that was all right, because he'd found the strength to do what he should have done weeks ago.

He would end things with Peyton.

ELEVEN

Cass was back. Peyton knew it as surely as she knew that the radio executives' convention began next week. The stack of notes covered with Cass's unmistakable handwriting sat squarely on her desk.

Peyton felt a pang of sadness. A few weeks ago he'd chastened her for hiding behind the "Top Kid" memo. Now he was doing the same. They were reduced to letters and reports, exactly how they'd communicated before. . . .

She sighed and began to read. Cass's comments were curt and to the point: people he'd spoken with, projects he'd manage during the convention, names of colleagues scheduled for other responsibilities. But there was no request to meet with him privately to discuss any final details, and no hint of affection. It was as if they had never made love, never shared the secrets of their hearts.

It was so unfair. Just when she'd finally come to realize what she wanted most, he snatched himself away. And her dreams of him, of them together, only sent Cass running faster. But dear God, she'd had a taste of heaven in Cass's arms and she wanted to go back. So much.

But she'd forced the issue, and now she had to live with the consequences. It was unfortunate that the consequences made her job more difficult, just because Cass didn't want to face her.

But he had no choice, really, she thought. Sooner or later they would have to talk it out and make some decision. But it would be uncomfortable until then, communicating by memo and generally tiptoeing around each other.

The door squeaked, an unnaturally loud sound in the quiet of the morning. Peyton jumped, startled, and looked up. Who could possibly be trying to find her at seven a.m.? She was never here this early.

The door swung open.

"Welcome home," she said softly.

Cass stood in the doorway, a thin notebook in his hand. The fluorescent light from the hall etched his features with harsh lines, accentuating yesterday's five o'clock shadow and the dark circles under his eyes. He looked bone-weary.

"How are you?" he asked.

"I missed you," she said simply.

"You could have called."

"Why? The station didn't require any decisions I couldn't make, and you needed to be away." She lifted the notes and tapped them on the desk to straighten the edges. "Were you successful?"

"Yes." He opened his mouth as if to say more, thought better of it and clamped it shut.

She would not pry. Cass would tell her about his trip if he wanted. She couldn't constantly beg for confidences. Cass was who he was. The sooner she accepted that, the better. "I'm glad," she said instead. "What's that? More stuff for the convention?"

He nodded and handed her the notebook that he'd come to deliver when he'd thought she wouldn't be here, when he wouldn't have to confront her. He opened his mouth again, and this time the words came out. "Since you're here, I'd like to talk about some other matters."

"Sure." She put the notebook aside and motioned Cass to a chair. Her gesture was calm, but her heart had begun to race. Was this it? The final confrontation that would send her on her way? Was he going to tell her how he wouldn't stand in the way of her future? How he couldn't really love her?

"You'll probably be hearing rumors of this during the convention, so I thought I'd better tell you up front," he began. Then he stopped, as if deciding how exactly to phrase his next words.

"Rumors? What's happened?" she asked, alarmed. Cass looked so haggard and drawn. Whatever it was, it had taken its toll on him. And as much as she wanted to comfort and console him, she knew she dared not. She had to let him work through it alone.

"Part of the reason I went to New York was to oversee a change in the ownership of WFKN," he said. "Once all the paperwork's filed with the FCC, I'll own the station outright."

"Outright?" This was a turn of events she hadn't expected.

"A consortium of buyers took over the station last summer. I was part of it. Now I've bought them out."

The truth slammed into her like a freight train and she breathed deeply, fighting the churning in her stomach. Cass *owned* the station. He was more than just her immediate supervisor. He signed the paychecks, he paid the bills, he held all the cards. Yet he'd never breathed a word of it! Not at the beginning, not as they'd come to know each other, not in public or private. He'd as good as lied to her.

Her wish to comfort him ran suddenly dry. "Congratulations." Her tone was caustic.

"You seem angry."

"How could you keep this a secret? We have a right to know exactly who we work for."

"It made sense. The buyout shook up the staff. You didn't need a celebrity owner along with the celebrity manager."

"Maybe not at first. But it's been months!"

Peyton inhaled, trying to keep her stomach where it belonged. The intimacy they'd once shared now seemed like nothing more than a sham. She didn't know the real Cass. If he kept the station ownership a secret— even from her—what other lies was he living?

"Why announce one change only to be followed by another?" Cass asked. It seemed a reasonable question, and Peyton fought down her unreasonable reaction. *Keep your temper*, she told herself.

"I'd always planned to buy out the consortium," Cass said, "and the staff will take the news better now that they know me. I'm committed to WFKN."

"*You're* committed to the bottom line." Peyton made it sound like a felony. "But what about the *people*? These are decent folks working here. They deserve to know who's really in charge."

She bit back a choked sob. "*I* deserve to know."

She took another deep breath, trying to steady herself with the oxygen she took in. All her recent choices flashed before her: hollow, worthless. She'd given herself—her body and her love—to a man who hadn't seen fit to tell her the truth. Heck, he couldn't even see that he'd been wrong.

"No one knew anything about this. Why should you?"

Peyton felt as if he'd struck her. Her temper erupted. "I'm not just another employee," she said. Her voice shook. "Not that I delude myself into thinking I could help you. I don't know if I ever could."

"Don't blame yourself. I wasn't a very good risk."

Something in the quiet resignation of his voice caught her attention. She studied him: the ashen skin drawn tight across his face, his eyes sunk deep in their sockets. He was tired and lonely, and he couldn't reach out for her. And she didn't dare reach for him.

Her anger snapped, leaving behind shards of sorrow. She'd failed him: in business and in love. She hadn't gotten through to him on either front.

What had she expected? That he would return from this trip eager for her friendship and her passion? That he would have magically overcome all his fears?

People didn't change overnight. Change took long hours of soul-searching, weeks and months to find the courage to face personal demons. She hadn't even resolved her own: her impatience was driving Cass away, and she couldn't steel herself to the painful inevitability of leaving him. So how could she expect Cass to have met and conquered his own ghosts, which ran so much deeper?

"It's not working, is it? I'm sorry, Cass." Despite her best efforts, her eyes glistened. Almost automatically she ran her fingers through her hair, tousling it.

Cass looked into the pain in Peyton's eyes and cursed himself. How had he brought that shining woman to this depth? Everything he'd touched for five years had turned out wrong, jinxed.

Coming home had been his last chance, a final act of faith. He'd taken himself out of the limelight, hoping, like a fool, that he could put his life in order.

He'd succeeded in some small measure. He had his home, some breathing room, a responsible staff. But there was only so much a man could do; after that it was best to keep out of the way of Fate.

But Fate had followed him, and she had a most perverse sense of humor. She'd sent Peyton to torment him just when he was struggling for his very existence. Fate couldn't let him manage one day at a time; no, she had to throw Peyton in his path. Now Peyton's face, her scent, her smile haunted his days and his dreams. She made him long for what he'd promised himself he'd never endure again. Love.

He'd struck back. He'd warned her, told her to stay away. He'd kept secrets where none were needed—the station ownership was just one of many. He'd lashed out when she was clearly right. None of it had worked. Peyton just kept on coming, with her straightforward love of life and her sweet-as-honey lips. And he'd been doomed.

The trip had at least brought him to his senses. He had to let Peyton go. She had to find and live her dreams without him, no matter what she thought she wanted. Dreaming was out of his reach. He wouldn't wrench it from her grasp as well.

"Regrets don't change reality, Peyton," he said stiffly. "You believe I kept important information from you and the staff. Do what you have to do."

"What I can't figure out is why. There's no good reason for this kind of secret." She spoke slowly, pensively.

"Why? Because I am who I am. I can't change that."

"Who are you, Cass?" The whisper caught him off guard, just like everything she did. "Just when I think I know you, you fool me again."

Who was he? A hopeless emotional cripple? A tired man, old before his time? A man with a past he couldn't shake and a future he was unwilling to seize?

He laughed, a short toneless bark that told Peyton everything—and nothing. "I'm a coward, Peyton. I'm still running away. I can't even turn and give you a decent fight."

"I don't want a fight." She rose and walked around her desk until she stood only inches from him. She reached to cup his face and pull it towards her. It was sandpaper rough, and it brought unbidden memories of a frigid night kept at bay with passionate heat. Their heat.

He'd felt the same way then: rough, edgy, hard like tiny sand crystals. She smoothed her fingertips across his skin. The raspy scratch of beard felt both familiar and foreign, as if Cass were two men. One had loved her so thoroughly that she trembled at the memory. One wanted nothing more than to forget every moment he'd spent with her.

Couldn't he see that he was splitting apart?

He's a chameleon, she thought. *One minute he's green and sensitive, the next he's as dark as night and just as terrifying. And like the chameleon, he's content to stay warm on his little rock, his world, changing to suit the moment but never looking ahead to the future.*

The future, she thought ruefully, that she wanted so very much. They could have it if they could move beyond the fear of the present. And the past.

"I don't want to fight," she repeated. "I just want to know why you've been trying to drive a wedge between us since the night we made love."

He looked at her, unflinching. "Because it was a mistake. Because I wanted you to realize that on your own."

"Why? Why was it wrong?" Her voice still shook, but this time it was from nerves, not anger.

"It meant too much to you."

"And it meant nothing to you?" She dropped her hand from his cheek, as if the touch of his face had blistered her fingers.

"You were warm, and we were good together. But—"

"I'm getting too close. I'm demanding too much."

Cass folded his arms across his chest and nodded, as if defying her to answer him with anything but rejection. She refused the challenge.

"No good, Cass," she answered boldly. "You're just running away again—from responsibility and from your feelings."

"Get out now, Peyton," he rasped. "Get out while you can still save yourself."

His tone forced her attention. He looked huge, sitting there—huge and dangerous, as if he were a tiger waiting to pounce on some very small prey. Her intuition flickered, and she knew that if she unchained his fury now, she would regret it.

Slowly she backed away, around the desk. Her legs found the edge of her chair and carefully she folded herself into it. Her movements were neat and spare, not requiring an extra second's exertion. She put all her energy into composing herself. Finally she spoke. "It's not over yet, Cass. This just isn't the time or the place. But mark my words—it's not over yet."

She bent over the notebook and began to read. A few moments later she picked up a pen to jot notes in the margin. She had to keep calm, no matter how out of control she felt. Calm, control—those were qualities Cass responded to.

What else did he respond to? The question snaked insidiously into her head, but she wouldn't dwell on the answer now. She wouldn't think about the moonlight playing on his skin, her hands doing the same, pleasuring him, igniting flames that ardor couldn't quench.

No! Neither would she think about how he'd hurt her with his words and his nodding agreement that she wanted too much. Because she didn't; she only wanted what she'd come to know and need.

The knowledge threatened to engulf her. Control! she thought fiercely and forced herself to reread the last paragraph. It didn't matter how much it hurt now; she had to maintain her composure.

She didn't acknowledge Cass when he rose and stalked out the door, silent and deadly as a cat. Only after he shut the door with the same frightening feline grace did she rest her head between her hands and moan.

The first day of the convention brought small crisis after small crisis: microphones that didn't work, meeting rooms without chairs, cold filets and warm salads. Peyton and the rest of the organizing committee scurried about like squirrels before autumn the entire day. Cass was nowhere to be found, although everything he said he'd do was, in fact, done. But he never seemed to be where he was needed when each small disaster arose.

"You're quite a trooper," Roger Forester said as Peyton resolved a problem with a missing hotel reservation. He'd come searching for her more than half an hour ago, but Peyton hadn't had a free moment to talk until now.

"I didn't think so many little things could go wrong," she said, sinking into a plush lobby sofa. It was hidden behind a lacquered Chinese screen and several large potted palms, giving them a measure of privacy in a public place.

"The important thing is that nobody noticed. That guy got his room, all the mikes are working, meals seem to be on schedule now—" Roger sat down beside her and smiled. "You've handled all this so well. I'm very impressed."

"Thank you." She colored a fraction, feeling the blush work its way up to her hairline. But in truth, Roger's approval was welcome. She'd gotten precious little of it elsewhere. More precisely, she'd gotten little from Cass.

"I've been so impressed, in fact," Roger continued, "that I've been wondering—have you ever thought about coming to New York?"

"Sure. Doesn't every radio type think about it?

"No," came Roger's casual reply. "Only the ones who are really serious about their careers."

"I guess I must be serious about it, then." She smiled. "Why do you ask?"

"What would you say to coming to work for me—at WCCB?"

"Excuse me?" She was too startled to respond properly, although she should have expected this—no one asked those kinds of questions without leading up to something big. Yet somehow she'd assumed this was a quiet moment of casual conversation between two rather harried colleagues.

Roger arched an eyebrow, as if to say, "Don't act so surprised."

"You're offering me a *job*?" Part of her said to grab it, but another part of her held her back.

"Why not? I need an assistant program director, and you're top notch. It's a match made in heaven."

"This is very flattering, but—" To her embarrassment, dismay tinged her voice, and Roger was too sharp to miss it. He would wonder why she was less than overjoyed at this chance.

She simply wasn't ready for New York, regardless of what part of her might say to the contrary. She hadn't finished her business with Cass.

"But what?" Roger ignored the overtones in her voice and named the salary. "It's a good offer. The responsibilities and the perks are nice."

As he outlined the job to her, Peyton began to feel radio fever boil in her blood as it hadn't since . . . since Cass had shut her out. Since her job had become routine and filled with memos, intermediaries and other neat tricks for avoiding Cass.

The more Roger said, the more the pull to fulfill her life's goal overwhelmed her. New York. National programming. A large staff of her own to manage. It was the kind of experience she needed before she bought that little station close to home.

Words failed her when Roger finished talking, but she knew he could see the excitement he'd kindled. It would have been hard to miss: eyes glowing, skin flushed, breathing shallow. Roger had terrific powers of persuasion.

"Wow," she said when she'd recovered. "It sounds great. It's just that—"

"Cass doesn't want to let you go," Roger interrupted, as if he'd known all along that she'd refuse. "I know. But he promised me I could ask."

"Cass knew?" She sounded more confident than she felt. "You discussed this with him?"

"Right after the last convention committee meeting. No harm in checking references, is there? He thinks you're ready for the big time."

Right after the last committee meeting! Right before they'd made love.

There had to be some connection. She thought about that night. The lovemaking had swept her off her feet, but Cass had been almost agitated when he'd invited her for supper. Everything had been so meticulously planned, as if . . .

Could Cass have been afraid of losing her, and used sex to try to keep her?

That was ridiculous, she told herself. Cass had to know that all he had to do was ask—and she'd stay with him.

Of course he did. But she'd scared him with all her twaddle about their future. He'd decided that she wasn't worth having—and he'd known that Roger would make her an offer too good to refuse. He'd held all the cards, and he was playing them like a master gambler.

All he'd had to do was turn cold. Peyton would despair of thawing him, of building a life together. Then Roger would come with his more-than-perfect offer—and Cass would be free.

Peyton shifted in her seat, struggling to keep a wave of nausea from overwhelming her. Cass wouldn't have stooped so low. It wasn't his style. He would have told her outright. Wouldn't he?

Hadn't he? Hadn't he told her to get out?

But he hadn't given her any reason. And she needed to hear—had to hear—that reason. She didn't believe that he didn't care. Whatever was moving him, it wasn't indifference. Fear, perhaps. A warped sense of duty, maybe. But not indifference.

She would put off this decision until she talked with Cass. She didn't expect it to be easy. This would be the catalyst, the final confrontation. It would either bring them together—or rip them apart.

She spoke slowly and carefully. "I'm flattered you've offered this to me. But I have to think about it."

"You're not sure?" Roger smiled. "I understand. Cass is a pretty powerful persuader. And with 'On Air America' about to become a reality, you've got some good opportunities here, too."

On Air *America*?

"Was that what that sudden trip to New York was all about? Syndication?" Again she spoke carefully, a tremendous understatement. "Cass doesn't always tell us everything."

"I bet I just said something I shouldn't," Roger said with a wry grin. "It seemed to be common knowledge in New York. I assumed you'd know."

Keep it light, she ordered herself. *Keep your feelings checked.* Peyton tried to tease him. "We both know what it means to assume. Don't worry about it."

"I'm still sorry. Not good protocol." He stood. Peyton followed his lead, although she wasn't quite sure how her legs supported her.

"It's okay. I'm glad to know the grapevine's still good for a tidbit or two."

"Peyton, think about this offer. I know Cass wants to keep you here, but New York can offer you a lot of advantages. And you won't find a better crew than at WCCB."

"I'd be lying if I said I wasn't tempted. I'll let you know before the convention's over."

They shook hands, and Peyton sank back into the sofa. She felt drained and empty, as if no emotion in the world could be enough to fill her again. First the station ownership, then the offer from Roger, and now "On Air America"! Cass had known it all along and never mentioned a word. It wasn't the kind of closeness she was used to—lies, secrets and silence.

Maybe they hadn't been close at all. What they'd shared might have been nothing more than a brief moment of physical release. She'd deceived herself into thinking it was intimacy, that she knew the real Cass when he didn't know himself, but. . . .

On Air America!

Peyton pulled inside herself, senses dulled. Around her hundreds of radio hands chattered and roamed, but she tuned them out. She had to think—and feel, feel the endless ache, the betrayal, and the anguish of losing what she'd come to desire with all her heart. She had to face her failure as woman, lover, and friend.

Roger had said Cass didn't want to lose her. Two weeks ago she might have believed him, but with his deceit Cass was showing her more surely than words could tell that he wanted her gone.

Peyton sat quietly, letting the waves of emotion scald her. Failure. That her greatest career offer should come on the heels of her failure with Cass struck her as bitterly ironic.

Slowly the pain subsided, and she tried to piece together the words she'd use with Cass. But she finally gave up. The words would come as they came, from her heart. She closed her eyes and leaned her head back on the edge of the sofa.

Some time later, two soft voices broke her meditation.

"I thought you were going to tell her about my offer,

prep her. She was completely surprised when I asked her.''

"I thought I was, too. But then I realized it's a decision she has to make. If I'd talked to her about it, well, I'm biased.''

"Of course you are. That's exactly why you should tell her how you feel.''

Silence, but Peyton had recognized the voices—Cass and Roger. Her eyes flew open. She ought to show herself, clear her throat at least, but instead she sat stock still, listening. They had to be talking about her.

"Are you going to offer her a chance to produce 'On Air America'?''

"Where'd you hear about *that*?''

"It's been all over the city for weeks. Everyone's talking about it. But I guess that news hasn't made it out here. I think I spilled the beans when I talked to Peyton.''

"What did you tell her?'' His tone was mild and restrained, but Peyton knew it for anger. She winced for Roger.

But Roger could handle it. His vigorous voice tolerated none of Cass's misplaced rancor. "I simply told her that she had a lot of opportunities here if she chose not to come to New York. Starting with 'On Air America'.''

"You had no right to mention that.''

"For crying out loud, Cass, it's all over the east coast. It's not my fault if you don't keep your people informed!''

"I don't believe in premature announcements. I wasn't sure until the contract was finished what I was going to do. It didn't make sense to get people excited about what might not happen.''

So it was true!

"You're the most cautious man I know. You never tell a soul until you've got a done deal. How you've made it this far in the radio racket I can't tell."

Cass—cautious? Not by a long shot. He'd been ruthless with her. He might choose to call it caution, but he was only fooling himself.

Peyton didn't catch Cass's next words. Then Roger spoke again.

"You know, most people figure your leaving New York was all part of some master plan to prove you could attract a national audience."

"Roger, you of all people should know better!" Now Cass really sounded angry.

"Of course I do. But you were too much for anything but the biggest markets until now. When you started working with Peyton, you got the right mix of topics and bingo! The national syndicates want you."

"I'm still not sure I want them." His anger seemed to have evaporated. "We only negotiated a six month contract. It's not even signed yet."

"When do you start?"

"Not until next spring. Assuming I can get all the right people in place."

"You've got the right people here! You're crazy to let Peyton leave."

"I won't make her decisions!" Cass thumped the lacquered screen that separated them. The vibration rustled the plants surrounding her. "I've made too many for other people. None of them ever turned out right."

"What are you talking about?" Roger sounded incredulous. "You're influencing her decision by *not* telling her how you feel! You've never been stupid, my friend. Why now?"

"I've thought this out very carefully, Roger." His defensive tone said, "Don't push."

But Roger, confident in the friendship of years, spoke bluntly. "You're not acting that way. You're not only letting Peyton leave, you're encouraging it. Explain that to me!"

Cass didn't respond, as if by ignoring Roger's question, it would somehow go away.

"It was that parole hearing, wasn't it? It tore you up again, seeing those punks that killed Katie. You couldn't save her, so you're not going to save yourself, either."

Oh, dear God! The pieces of the puzzle—Cass's cold remoteness, his denial of all they were together—clicked into place in Peyton's mind. Cass had gone to New York to face down Katie's murderers, and he hadn't so much as hinted at it. But what nightmares *that* would resurrect!

"You're just going to let your second chance get away, aren't you?" Roger demanded.

"There's no such thing as a second chance, Roger," Cass said stiffly. "You only get one, and mine's gone."

"You're kidding yourself. Any fool can see that you not only got a second chance, you *made* one. You broke out of the rat race. And you fell in love. But some misguided, guilt-ridden part of you thinks that's wrong. So instead of living your love, you're busy denying it."

Love? Peyton held her breath, and her heart beat an irregular syncopated rhythm. Roger knew Cass and knew him well. He would recognize a change in Cass's emotional state. Could he possibly be right? Did Cass love her?

She had very nearly accepted that he couldn't. Every word, every action since her ill-timed declaration bespoke a man unsure of his emotions. And her one-sided devotion wasn't enough. All that had remained was to plan a decent burial for her feelings.

Did Cass love her? Could love, frail with doubt, explain his silences and half truths? Could it keep her here, keep her trying?

With a hope spun of dreams and desires, Peyton knew it could. It was crazy of her, but she wanted to give Cass the second chance he would refuse himself. He only had to let her know he wanted it, too.

She took a long, deep breath, scarcely able to exhale as she waited for Cass to speak. A fragile optimism took tentative flight, like a baby gull learning to swoop among the clouds. Cass might deny his feelings to her but surely not to his best friend. Roger would encourage him to see the truth, and act on it.

But Cass's next words were like a hunter's arrow, piercing her soaring bird of hope and sending it hurtling to earth, bruised and broken.

"Roger, I've told you and I've told her: I am not a man for love. I don't love her—I don't love anyone."

"You liar. Why won't you believe what you feel?"

"Love died a long time ago. There's nothing left. The sooner you and Peyton realize this, the sooner we can all get on with our respective business."

She should have known. He might have succumbed, but that was not love. Desire, yes. Passion, certainly. Warm physical release, absolutely. But love? Cass refused to believe in love. How could he experience what he didn't believe in?

It was time to stop deceiving herself.

Cass had no choice; he had to remain here. But Peyton didn't. And Cass's plan, she thought ruefully, if that's what it was, had worked. She would leave him alone with his bitterness and his fear. The pleasures and affection they'd shared would linger as a sorry memory, and Cass would fortify his defenses against even that happening again. He would never find that second chance.

She couldn't waste any more energy worrying about a man who didn't worry about himself. She knew what she had to do. With a small hiccup, she rose and walked out from behind the screen.

"Cass, Roger." Peyton paused a moment to center herself, calm her jangling nerves. Cass's face was twisted with—distress? diffidence? apprehension? She couldn't quite read it before it disappeared into smooth blankness.

"Peyton," both acknowledged her arrival. Roger was overly bright, as if concerned that she might find him and Cass in a disagreement. Cass was now inscrutable.

Somehow his imperturbability made her angry. She let the feeling settle around her like armor: cool, controlled and well-directed. Oddly enough, she had no thought of revenge. She only wanted the strength to finish with Cass.

"I'm glad you're together so I'll only have to say this once." Like a knight on a quest, she plunged ahead. "Cass, Roger has offered me a position at WCCB. I've decided to accept."

"Are you sure?" Roger spoke first. "There are a lot of good opportunities here."

"Rescinding your offer?" she spoke calmly, squelching the momentary flash of alarm. Roger was Cass's friend, and he thought Cass was in love with her. He might try to force Cass's hand by—

"No, no. You just haven't had long to think about this."

"Radio is made on quick decisions. I know what I need to do."

Cass was silent. Peyton thought she saw his face cloud with—concern? fear? Just as quickly, it cleared, returning to impassivity.

"Cass, I won't leave you in the lurch," she said. "Roger told me I don't need to report until January. That should be plenty of time to train a new PD."

Cass still said nothing. Couldn't he even say good luck, that the station would miss her? She was giving him his out, and he couldn't even wish her well? The icy cool of her anger flared brightly, and her next words cut like a surgeon's scalpel.

"You shouldn't have any trouble filling my position: hordes of producers want a shot at working on a national program like 'On Air America,' with a personality like you. And this time you can keep your distance. I only wish I had."

There, that had done it. Cass's face went one, no, two shades paler and his eyes glazed with a sheen of ice.

"Roger, would you excuse us?" he said swiftly. "Peyton and I have some unfinished business before she storms Manhattan."

Roger nodded to each of them and left.

"I suppose you think I deserved that last remark," Cass said. Peyton watched him warily, unable to gauge his next words. She'd unleashed his tiger. "Not that I care. I just wonder why you brought Roger into our private little mess."

"You already had." Peyton's voice was as brittle as parchment. "He talked to you about me. And you never so much as hinted that I'd get the chance to go to New York. My big dream, and it was just one more secret to you, like owning 'FKN and 'On Air America' and—"

"I had my reasons for keeping quiet. None of my

employees knew anything about any of this. Why should you?''

Peyton felt as if he'd struck her. "So we're back to that. Stupid me. I thought I was more than an *employee*," she said bitterly.

You were, he thought. But he couldn't reveal that to her. She had to move ahead, make a life for herself. She wanted too much, so much more than he could give. He wouldn't risk her coming to hate him for making her settle for less than she deserved. Let her come to hate him now, with the hot fury of rejection. It was preferable to her learning bit by bit to despise him for his weaknesses.

But God, he hurt. And if he didn't find his voice soon, Peyton, with her all-seeing eyes, would know he wasn't as determined as he wanted her to believe.

"We haven't worked. I've tried to tell you but you wouldn't listen. It's time to grow up now, get on with your career and your life."

"Grow up? You're the one who needs to grow up. You're the one who wanted to pick up the pieces of your life. You're the one who wanted to rebuild trust in your fellow human. At least that's what you said."

"And it hasn't worked. I've made a mess of everything I've touched. I know that. And I want you out of here before I hurt you any more."

"Before you hurt *me*? Look at yourself, Cass! You were right!" she shot back. "You *are* a coward—so busy insulating yourself from others and the past that you can't live in the present. I see a man with such a warped sense of duty that he'd rather send me away than take a chance on loving me!"

"I'm not sending you away! You're free to stay."

"Right. In an atmosphere so uncomfortable that neither of us can function!"

"Sarcasm doesn't become you, Peyton."

"What do you care?" Her words dripped bitter pain, and she hoped Cass felt every drop. Because she certainly did, and it was burning a hole inside her. A big gaping hole that she would despair of ever filling.

I needed you! she cried silently.

"Peyton, I can't be what you want."

She pushed her fingers through her hair and looked at him for a long time. In the cold, pale yellow of the afternoon sun, Cass appeared tired and sorrowful— perhaps even more so than she.

All her misplaced affection resurged. Despite the pain, despite Cass's incomprehensible actions, she still ached for him. She wanted to hold him, to soothe away the agony that had driven him to deny her.

But it was no good. Peyton shivered beneath the weight of her winter tweeds and admitted defeat. Cass couldn't be deterred; he was set on her leaving. So why was she fighting so hard? In a way, New York was what she wanted, too.

But she grieved over her inability to touch him as he'd touched her. She couldn't bring the shining lights to his life as he had done for her. She couldn't make him rejoice in living as he had done for her. She couldn't . . .

She felt what was left of her anger crack and splinter, leaving only regret behind. Regret that she hadn't been stronger and more persuasive. Regret that she couldn't bind up the past and heal him.

She'd let him down. She'd let herself down.

"I'm so sorry," she whispered. "So very sorry. I'll go now." She seized his hand and pressed it tightly for a second, then dropped it and wheeled away.

But Cass had already seen the glint of tears. Dear God, what had he done?

_____ TWELVE _____

"Surprise!"

"How can you leave us?"

"We're really going to miss you!"

The tenth floor conference room had been transformed for a surprise farewell party for Peyton. A long table piled with food sat against one wall, and helium-filled balloons decorated the ceiling. Two upholstered conference chairs were stacked with bright packages. Her colleagues had draped a huge Mylar banner wishing her "Good-bye and Good Luck!" across the back wall.

Nearly everyone was here: Sally, of course, the day and late night/weekend crews, the marketing staff, her interns. Peyton was touched. Despite the burden that would fall on everyone's shoulders after she was gone, everyone wished her well. They seemed genuinely happy and excited for her.

"The evening shift promised to stop by after nine," one of her interns said.

"How long have you been plotting this?" Peyton said, batting a loose balloon back towards the ceiling.

"Since before Christmas. You can't imagine how glad we were when you left for a week in Detroit!" Sally laughed. "We did a pretty good job, didn't we?"

"I'm really touched."

Peyton spent the next several hours talking and reliving the past four years with the people who'd been like family. The evening was warm and familiar, like the crazy gifts they'd brought: bumper stickers and ball caps from the marketing staff, a signed Ohio State football from the sports crew, outtake tapes from the engineers.

"You guys are wonderful," Peyton said warmly as she accepted another heartfelt toast. "I'm going to miss you all so much!"

"So why don't you stay?"

The real reason was too painful. Cass—who didn't love her. Cass—who didn't trust her. Cass—who refused to budge from her mind.

Or her heart.

She held back the flicker of anguish and laughed. "I can't pass up a chance like this. You should be glad I'm going. Pretty soon I'll be famous, and I'll get jobs for everyone!"

"Yeah, yeah!" her friends cheered. But beneath the merriment ran a current of sadness. Peyton's leaving was inevitable now; the final good-byes had been said, the final good wishes expressed. The "For Sale" sign was up on her front lawn and the movers were coming tomorrow to pack the last of her belongings and transport them to her new home. Everything was as it should be.

Except Peyton didn't see it that way.

None of this had happened as she'd wanted. Her leaving was not so much a victory as a defeat: having failed with Cass, she had no choice but to go. And since she and Cass had been so careful to keep the depth of their relationship detached from the station, no one suspected that her leaving was anything more than an enviable promotion. They had no idea how much this hurt.

What choice did she have? Airing her parting with Cass might undermine his authority for a while, but it would change nothing. She would still be gone. Better to leave with her dignity intact.

The party was breaking up. Surrounded by the deep friendship of people she'd worked with and cried with for so long, Peyton said her last good-byes and thank-yous.

"Thanks, Cindy. You've been terrific!"

"Of course I'll write, Phil. I know you'll want the scoop about life in the big city."

"Jackie, I'll be glad to hire you when I have an opening on my staff. So if you want to come to New York . . ."

"Good-bye, Glen! Thanks again!"

Time to move on. Peyton realized that. But she'd never expected it to hurt so much.

The night was bitterly cold and utterly cheerless. The new moon gave little light, and the street lamp down the block was black. But still Cass waited near the brick street, as he had for the past hour. He had to see Peyton one last time.

The past two weeks had whipped by. He'd endured them stoically, tamping down every stray emotion, re-fusing to admit—what? Remorse, regret, shame . . . He wasn't sure.

But tonight, alone in the studio, with half the staff already gone to Peyton's party and the rest leaving as soon as the shift was over, it had finally hit him. Peyton was leaving.

Because of him.

She'd loved him. But the knowledge did nothing to warm him. She might love him, but she wouldn't stay with him. He'd pushed and pushed, and he'd finally driven her away.

It was what he'd wanted. So why was he here? Couldn't he allow her the dignity of leaving in peace? Did he have to drive the idea home one last time that he couldn't—wouldn't—let her in his life? Did he think that reviewing that unpleasant lesson would make leaving any easier for her?

Did he think it would make her leaving any less painful for him?

He stamped up and down the sidewalk, unwilling to take shelter in his Jeep. He wanted the cold, wanted to feel its icy whistle through his parka. It *felt* right. It chilled his soul, freezing the agony that refused to stay tamped down.

Pain gnawed at his gut. *Well*, he mocked himself, *you came home to feel again. And you ought to hurt! You're killing the best thing that's happened to you in five years. And you have no choice.*

Cass saw Peyton's Mustang rumble slowly down the uneven street, and he positioned himself in her driveway. He wanted her to see him as she pulled in so she wouldn't think he was some sort of lunatic. He didn't need to add fear to his arsenal.

All the way home, Peyton had grieved. Her pleasant, full life in Columbus was over. And while New York was a longed for, hoped for challenge, it still came on the heels of personal failure. Only time and hard work could expunge the sense of loss.

This is the last time I'll drive home here, she thought

nostalgically as she maneuvered the little vehicle into her driveway.

Then she saw Cass's outline in the stark light of her headlamps. Despite the warmth of the car's heater and her down coat, she grew numb. She hadn't expected to see him again.

Cass was nothing if not unpredictable. But why now?

They had barely spoken since the convention, communicating only in writing when it was absolutely necessary. He hadn't attended the party, although his absence would surely be the subject of later speculation. Nor had he signed the five-foot farewell card shaped like a radio transmitter tower. It was as if by refusing to acknowledge her, he could deny that she'd ever had a role in his life.

He wasn't denying her now. He'd searched her out, waited for her return. Nervous, she killed the engine.

Cass came around to her door and opened it. Peyton felt winter's biting breath suck away her own. Or maybe it was Cass. He could still make her breathe in ragged gasps.

"Why?" she asked helplessly. "Why couldn't you just let me go?"

"I had to see you again. Tell you—" he stopped. The whole exercise of waiting for Peyton had been futile. The glint in her eyes told him she abhorred him, hated the arrogance that had brought him here so late on her last night. What had he wanted from her? Forgiveness? A blessing? There could be no peace, no forgiveness. Not for him.

He was too fundamentally damaged. He couldn't love her back. He couldn't trust her, not even to share the most basic facts about himself. Such as owning her place of employment. Such as being able to fulfill her biggest dreams. Such as not wanting to destroy her.

"Tell me what, Cass?" Her voice carried on the wind, sharp and insistent.

"That I—" What? That he loved her? No. That wasn't possible. That he was sorry? Perhaps, but why reopen wounds that had begun to knit together?

"Cass, I've never known you to be tongue-tied." A hint of annoyance wafted on the wind. "It's late. We have lives to lead tomorrow. What did you have to say?"

"I wanted to wish you well. To tell you I know you'll do fine."

Peyton considered his answer. Cass was not given to impulsive gestures, and his waiting was too impulsive for a simple fond farewell.

Cass had no right to intrude now. Not while she was still gathering strength for the next few weeks.

"You came here and waited I don't know how long to tell me that?" she demanded. "Why not write me a memo?"

The barb hit home. In the distortion of frozen breath, Peyton thought she saw Cass wince. Then he straightened, extended his hand and pulled Peyton from the car. The pressure of his hand through his leather gloves was unrelenting and strong. It matched the intensity of his eyes, the restrained power of his carriage.

The car door slammed with a hollow thud, closing off one escape.

"You never write memos about sensitive subjects."

His familiar voice enveloped her, and she fought the feeling of warmth it involuntarily fueled. Not tonight. Not ever. She'd made her decision, as he'd made his. Nothing could change her mind.

"So let me help you *say* it. Say, 'Good-bye, Peyton. Good luck, Peyton. We'll miss you, Peyton.' That's not so hard, is it?"

"Not if that were what I'd come to say."

"What *did* you come to say? Why don't you say it and get out?" she asked impatiently. But the impatience was only a mask for a deeper river of anguish. It threaded its way through her voice, through her body. Cass must have detected it in the stiffened way she held herself, unyielding to his touch. He dropped her hand.

"Do you hate me so much?" he asked. Hate, he acknowledged ruefully, could be a strong antidote to pain. To love. If she left Columbus hating him, perhaps the pain wouldn't destroy her, the way it nearly had him. She might be able to love again. Someday.

That was what he'd come for. To reassure her that their failure wasn't hers at all, that it was he who couldn't give. Or trust. Or—

"I don't hate you." She spoke softly, and Cass had to strain to catch her words. "But I can't live like this: economizing my own feelings, pretending I don't feel their overwhelming intensity. And you can't live *with* them.

"So I have to go, Cass. It's too late for any other solutions." She pulled her keys from her coat pocket and walked towards the front door.

"I see that now," he muttered grimly. "But Peyton—"

"Yes?" She cocked her head so she could see him. Her face, pale in the dimness of night, was engraved with proud distress.

What am I doing? Cass thought. *Why can't I simply let her leave?*

Because, a tiny interior voice scolded him, *Peyton means more to you than anyone. And instead of doing the right thing, you torment her and call it reassurance. Well, you can reassure all you want, but she'll still blame herself because you won't face the truth.*

Cass shook away the voice in one long stride. He stood beside Peyton under the eaves and captured her shoulders between his hands.

"Don't blame yourself, Peyton. It was nearly always me."

"God, you're an arrogant SOB," she shouted. "You can't even share the credit for us going wrong!" Peyton shivered as his strong fingers gripped her more tightly.

"I suppose I am. Just add it to the list of reasons to get out now."

Peyton heard the hopelessness and bitterness that accompanied Cass's words, and suddenly knew that her pain was miniscule by comparison. She was only suffering a broken heart.

Cass was suffering a broken life.

She had to leave something behind for him: a powerful memory that he wouldn't be able to keep out of his mind or a shred of truth for comfort in the chill days ahead—truth that he would inevitably try to deny himself.

But it didn't matter. It was her parting gift to him, the man who'd brought sunshine and joy and sorrow to her all at once. Deep within herself, she knew she was stronger because of it. But Cass, ah Cass . . .

Cass would survive. But survival without love would be cold and lonely indeed.

"I meant everything I said," she whispered. "I loved you."

"Peyton, I didn't mean—"

"Shh." She ran her fingers down the soft wool of his coat, remembering the softness of skin and the tautness of corded muscle that lay beneath. An icy tremor skated down her spine. Slowly she turned towards him and stood on her tiptoes.

"I wasn't kidding about this, either," she said, raising her gaze to meet his. Quietly, gently, she touched her lips to his cheek. He tasted sharp and dry.

Cass moved his head a fraction. Without knowing exactly how, Peyton was suddenly kissing him on the lips.

He responded. His arms wrapped around her more tightly, gathering her up like a bundle of wheat.

The kiss that had started out gentle and quiet became neither. Cass's mouth covered hers. She kissed him deeply, branding the memory of her on his soul. He would not forget her.

Peyton's senses began to crackle and burn. Her ears, hypersensitive in the silent night, heard every rasping breath Cass took. He was breathing faster now, short, shallow pants that told her he hadn't forgotten how the world ignited when they were together. His skin was still pungent and dry, but his lips were warm from the liquid friction of Peyton's caresses.

She nipped and nuzzled. She teased and tugged. She unwound her arms from his firm embrace and encircled his neck, and Cass pulled her body closer to him.

Her senses throbbed. She felt his heated breath wrap itself around her face before it condensed into the frosty air. She could feel the exquisite pressure of Cass's tongue as it probed, demanding surrender. She could feel the heat of her blood as it pounded in her veins, begging for release.

It was like their first kiss: soul-searing, passionate beyond experience, and wildly, totally wrong.

With a start, Peyton realized what she'd begun, and she was ashamed. Her own brand of arrogance had tripped her up again. She couldn't just let Cass go, either: she'd had to singe every corner of her mind and body with the memory of him. He might not forget her, but neither would she be able to forget him.

She let herself go slack. Her arms dropped to his shoulders, and she pulled them back cautiously.

"You see?" she said plaintively. "I try for platonic and all I get is passion."

"It does seem to be our strong suit."

"I have to go now. I have an early day tomorrow." She walked three steps to her doorstep and pushed the house key into the lock. The door opened silently.

"Good-bye, Peyton. Good luck."

"I guess two out of three's not bad, huh?" She shut the door behind her.

"I'll miss you, Peyton," he whispered to the door.

January 20

Dear Sal,

Well, here I am. New York is nothing like I expected. It's crazy, it's full of life, and I never know who or what I'm going to meet on the streets: the hot dog vendor, the chestnut salesman, the crazy street preachers. This place just teems!

My apartment is a sardine can compared to what I had in Columbus, but by New York standards I'm living in luxury. I've got a large studio and *most* of my stuff fits. The bookshelves make a nice wall so my bed sits in an alcove by itself. But I had to put some of my furniture in storage, so I don't have a desk or much of a kitchen set. Oh, well, who has time to cook?

I did find room for the sleeper sofa, so you and everyone back in Columbus are welcome to visit. I'm in a great location on the Upper East Side— twenty minutes to work on the subway.

Gotta run and catch that subway! Love to Jack and the kids! Hope the new job is working out! Write soon.

Peyton

January 31

Hi, Sal!

Sorry it's taken so long to get back to you. I ought to just call, but I spend so much time on the phone that I can't bear to talk after hours. Besides, letters are so much more permanent.

The new job's *tough*: lots of late hours and crazy producers. It's not just the headaches of producing a single show and trying to keep the radio station running. It's bigger. I'm handling the production and distribution of ten syndicated programs, and most of the time I don't know if I'm coming or going. Last week the satellite feed went down, and I had some wild problems with obscene callers.

I've developed a few new systems to track potential trouble, but this kind of work is always going to be putting out other people's fires. I don't know—I seem to be having second thoughts. Crisis management isn't as much fun as I remembered.

Some good news: my house sold this week. So I'm looking for a little co-op to buy into. I've been poking around all the nicer neighborhoods, where there are some great places. But ouch, the prices!

Tell the gang howdy from me.

Love,
Peyton

February 16

Dear Sal,

I warn you, this is going to be a cranky letter. So put it down now if you're not up for complaints.

Where can I start? How about with the fact that

I've had no heat in my apartment for two days? The furnace went out on Sunday, and the super hasn't been able to get it repaired yet. It doesn't help that we're in the middle of one of the coldest winters on record. I've been wearing my coat indoors to keep warm.

My car was vandalized. Everyone's been telling me to get rid of it and ride the subway, but I wanted to keep it for a while. I've been storing it in a garage, but that wasn't safe enough. The convertible top was slashed. They tried to pry out my stereo but all they succeeded in doing was smashing my dash—to the tune of $1,300. Can't wait to see what that does to my insurance rates.

My boss, Roger, informed me today that we're going to add two new shows to the national syndicate. That's two more balls to juggle. My staff is terrific, but there's only so much you can delegate. The rest of the responsibility is mine.

Sometimes it just overwhelms me. I'm good enough, but sometimes I wonder if it's all worth it. After all, I don't want to work here forever—and a lot of what I'm doing won't ever apply to a small station in the midwest.

I have to keep my sights on that—I'm not going to be here forever. But sometimes it seems that way. I've only been here six weeks, but it feels like six years.

I really miss you. I miss Columbus and WFKN and shopping at City Center and eating Bremen Brats at Rainer's. And if you want the truth, I miss Cass, too. I didn't know it would still hurt so much when I didn't see him day after day. It's the craziest thing I've ever done, falling in love with someone who can't love me back. I thought distance—and time—would help, but I can't shake my feelings. I suppose he's doing fine. I never meant much to him.

Gosh, Sal, I'm sorry for dumping on you. This letter's been a real downer. But what are best friends for? Thanks for listening. I'll be more cheerful next time, I promise.

Love to everyone,
P.

Friday

Dear Peyton,

I know Federal Express with Saturday delivery is extravagant, and I probably shouldn't meddle, but you have to hear this tape. It's last night's edition of "On Air Columbus." It's Cass and Jane Thomas, the psychologist who wrote *The Intimacy Trap*. (I hear the operations manager's been doing the scheduling for the show. I guess that's just what Cass deserves.)

Anyway, I hear that he and Cass had an awful fight about whether Dr. Thomas would appear. I think it's one of the best shows Cass has done, but he fought it like wildfire. And it makes me think your leaving 'FKN was premature.

If you want a little armchair analysis, I think Cass misses you badly. The biggest clue is this tape. But according to all my sources at 'FKN, Cass has been a bear—polar, grizzly and brown all rolled into one. He harasses the sales reps, the engineers are ready to draw blood, and he's made no effort to interview anybody for your old job. For a man who owns the station, he's not interested in the proper details. And this interview shows why.

Throw it away if I'm out of line, but the part of me that believes in happily ever after says that Cass is crying for you.

Love,
Sally

P.S. The new job's great. More on that later!

Peyton ran her fingers around the tape's hard plastic case. It was a talisman of Columbus, and she hesitated to throw it away. But what could she possibly accomplish by listening to it? A single tape would solve none of their problems. It couldn't lessen her foolish desire for Cass—a desire that distance and time hadn't quenched. It couldn't make Cass into a man who allowed deep feelings to surface, who could trust her with his heart. It couldn't give Peyton the patience she needed to wait for him.

More to the point, Cass would still be there and she would still be here. There was nothing left for her in Columbus: her house was sold, and her job would soon be filled. Besides, she had responsibilities to Roger and WCCB.

She hefted the tape once, twice, and then pitched it into the trash can by the sofa. It landed with a thud. She could forgive Sally for trying, but she'd never forgive herself if she listened. Hearing Cass's voice again would be too painful.

She puttered around the apartment for the next hour. It was already late; she'd had a full day at the station trying to tie up loose ends she could never finish during the week. She couldn't deal with Cass right now.

She fixed tuna salad for dinner, washed the dishes and took a shower. Movement helped her forget what waited in the wastebasket. But as soon as she stopped, her eyes would stray to the wicker basket at the end of the sofa.

Peyton made a pot of coffee and curled up in the rocking chair with a mystery novel. But the story, with its intricate plot and carefully wrought clues, failed to hold her interest. Rocking and reading weren't movement enough. Peyton kept losing her place as she gazed at the wicker wastebasket. It was as if the tape were calling her, demanding that she give Cass a fair hearing.

She shook her head, put the book aside and retrieved the cassette. She would undoubtedly regret it, but Sally's ploy had worked. Peyton would listen one last time.

She sat on the floor, flipped the cassette in the tape deck and pressed the play button. the "On Air Columbus" theme lasted a few seconds, then Cass's voice filled the room.

"My guest tonight is Dr. Jane Thomas, who's here to talk about her new book, *The Intimacy Trap*."

His voice was everything she'd remembered: smoky, dark, like a sultry embrace in the moonlight.

She didn't have to listen to the words for them to mesmerize her. The cadence and the timbre of his voice were enough to send her imagination reaching back to recreate those magic moments together: murmurs and sighs, kisses and long, stroking caresses. Her face began to flush and her whole body felt warm and tingly.

She bit her lower lip and reached for the stop button.

No. She would hear this out, face the devil one more time so she could put him away forever. She simply hadn't counted on it being so hard.

"Dr. Thomas, what's the theme of your book? What is the intimacy trap?"

"It's the idea that everyone wants and needs intimacy in their relationships. That's just not true. For some people, intimacy and gut-level trust are just too much. They can't cope with it—and they shouldn't have to."

What had Sally been thinking of? This woman was espousing Cass's personal philosophy—that intimacy was a sham. Sally knew this was the very issue that had driven Peyton to New York.

"A lot of psychologists say that intimacy is the most fundamental human need," said Cass.

"That's just not so. A lot of other needs are far more basic: food, clothing, sexual release. Intimacy is a by-product of our post-industrial society. We no longer have to worry about where our next meal is coming from or that the saber-tooth tiger is going to attack. So we find other things to worry about. Intimacy is one. And a lot of people can't deal with it."

"But those people are hiding themselves away from the truly wonderful thing that intimacy can be!"

"Who's to say that intimacy is such a great thing? So often it leads to heartache, broken marriages, and broken relationships."

"But a relationship is so much better if the people are intimate!"

Peyton stabbed the tape player's stop button. She couldn't believe it. Cass—defending intimacy? Defending relationships? It wasn't possible. Yet it was his voice, his show.

And he certainly sounded convincing.

He must be playing devil's advocate, keeping the topic controversial. He couldn't be giving his real opinion. Peyton hit the play button and the tape started again.

"Cass, you seem an odd sort to have these opinions about intimacy. You have a reputation as a hard-edged interviewer. I was a little bit worried about being a guest on 'On Air Columbus.' Where did you get this soft center that believes in intimacy?''

There was a long pause on the tape. Peyton winced. Dead air was a nightmare to be avoided at all costs. Finally, Cass responded slowly.

''I had a very good marriage several years ago. Before my wife died, she taught me a lot about love.''

That was true enough. And Peyton could sense an undercurrent of honesty in Cass's words.

''Fair enough. But you haven't gotten involved since then, have you? Intimacy is too hard to sustain.''

Again there was another long pause. ''Actually, I recently broke up with a woman who also taught me a lot about love and respect.'' He laughed, but to Peyton is sounded hollow. ''But I was too busy practicing what you preach about defending oneself from the violation of intimacy. But somehow, now that it's too late, I've come to believe in it after all.''

The tape droned on, but Peyton heard little of it. Her heart thundered in her ears. Cass believed she had taught him something about love! Love—the very emotion he'd disdained.

Weakly, she pulled herself onto the sofa. So what now? Maybe she had taught him something. But if so, why had he said nothing? Why had he let her go? And if he hadn't discovered the truth until after she'd left, why hadn't he called or written since then?

She sighed as she unraveled the truth. Silence was Cass's style. He'd kept quiet about owning the station, about his syndicated program, about Roger's offer. Naturally he wouldn't talk about this. Only through the strangely public anonymity of the show could he reveal his feelings—and even then, he couldn't expect Peyton to have heard his confession.

No, if he found that he'd been wrong, he wouldn't come looking for her. He would accept his own bad decision, a consequence of his own choice.

And Peyton herself? She, too, had a choice—to live with a bad decision or, having heard Cass's declaration, to try again.

She had nothing left to lose. She picked up the telephone and began to dial.

_____ THIRTEEN _____

In the twilight realm between sleep and waking, Cass heard the church bells. High and low they tolled, marking the passage of his life: the Sundays of his youth spent in Bible school; the innumerable Sundays he'd spent establishing his career; the day he'd buried Katie, their mournful dirge clanging home his double grief; and the most recent bells of joy, quiet since Peyton's departure.

He tossed on the sofa, willing the bells to be silent. But they chimed on mercilessly, rousing him to waking.

Then there weren't bells at all, only the telephone ringing insistently. Half awake, Cass stumbled across the room. By the time he picked up the receiver, the answering service had taken the call.

God, what time was it? This was a hell of a way to spend Saturday night, falling asleep watching some sappy fifties' love story on TV. But what other choice did he have? No one at work wanted to come near him after hours; he'd been an unholy terror and he knew it.

His friends in Ashville knew too much of his history.

Their friendships were colored with memories of Katie and their understanding of the agony he'd endured reconciling himself to her death. They'd helped enough. He couldn't ask them to hear him out again over Peyton. He had to deal with this by himself.

Thursday's on-the-air confession had stunned him. When he'd skimmed *The Intimacy Trap* to come up with questions for the interview, he'd agreed with just about everything Jane Thomas had to say. So he'd been astonished to hear views he hadn't known he held coming from his mouth.

He loved Peyton. When had he come to that conclusion? He, who hadn't believed in love, who had refused to give it the power to hurt him again, was in love. When had he discovered that he craved intimacy, that he yearned for peace and stability, that he ached for Peyton's warm, pliant body next to his?

Paradoxically, he'd come home to make peace with himself. And in doing so, he'd stumbled on love. Peyton had woven herself into the fabric of his life—so that church bells could toll the delightful hours they'd spent together.

But Cass, fearful of loving and losing again, of seeing Peyton's love turn to sorrow and ultimately abandonment, had forced her away. Just like Katie.

He'd found no peace in Peyton's absence, though. Ironically, he was lonelier than he'd been before he'd come back. Work had lost its flavor—it was all he could do to hold his temper and keep from lashing out over insignificant details. Home had become a prison—even walking the perimeter of the farm failed to calm him.

Despite his best efforts, he'd fallen helplessly, hopelessly in love. It was only after he'd driven Peyton away that he'd been forced to admit to himself what he'd so long denied—once again love had found him, branded him, and torn him apart.

But Jane Thomas, with her ridiculous ideas about intimacy, had put everything in perspective. He needed Peyton. Needed her like a man needs a woman—for better and for worse.

But could he convince her?

He'd convinced her of plenty before she'd gone: convinced her that she meant nothing to him; convinced her that he'd kept secrets from her, secrets she'd had a right to know; convinced her that he'd withheld the truth of his feelings from her.

What made him think that his own revelations would be welcome now? It might well be too late.

He padded upstairs to his bedroom and went to his dresser. He opened the top drawer, pulled out a small silver picture frame and carried it to bed.

He sprawled on his stomach and stared at the photo for a long time.

"Oh, Katie, love, I've made a mess of things, haven't I?" He sighed. "I couldn't get it right with you, and I really blew it with Peyton.

"You tore me up when you left. When you didn't show up at the counselor's office, I thought you'd changed your mind, that you'd truly given up on me. And then when I saw what those kids did to you . . .

He laid the picture on the bed and looked down at his dead wife's face, young, carefree, full of encouragement. "So what do you think, Kate? Would we have made it? That's what I need to know. If you think we might have, if there was still hope . . . at the end . . . then maybe it's worth trying to convince Peyton."

He gazed at the picture, remembering their early days, the happy times. They'd been poor students, but that hadn't stopped them from sharing simple things:

walks in the woods, cups of cocoa, bouquets of wild-flowers in the spring. It had been the sharing that had mattered. It had been the sharing that he'd forgotten.

Could they have found those people again, weathered the storm of Katie's discontent, rebuilt their marriage? Cass shook his head, unsure.

Then he heard the answer in his head, a laughing, twinkling lilt he hadn't heard in years. Katie's own voice, before their troubles.

Well, you took your time asking me that, silly man! The voice turned softer, gentler. *Of course we would have made it. We both wanted to, and in the end, we were ready to do what we needed to save us. We loved each other. It's just that sometimes,* her voice grew firmer in his mind, *I had to be a bit . . . dramatic to get your attention.*

Katie? Or just his subconscious, giving him a new glimpse of his past, a new perspective, the freedom to break out and try again?

The voice spoke again, a whisper dimmed by time and memory. *I loved you. Always. And now it's time to remember how love works, how it worked for us, how it can work for you and Peyton.*

Go and get her, Cass. Bring her home. Make her happy.

And Cass. The voice was fading now. *You'd better do something dramatic. You've got a lot of convincing to do.*

Cass pressed the picture to his cheek swiftly. "I'll make you proud of me," he whispered.

He took one last look at the photograph, then re-placed it in the drawer. He rummaged further and found paper and pen. Quickly he scratched a list of things he had to do before he left.

The telephone rang again, but Cass, his brain on fire,

refused to be distracted. Let the answering service get it. If it were important, they'd beep him.

"No, thanks, no message." Peyton replaced the telephone receiver in its cradle. Why had she thought Cass would be home on a Saturday night? She'd even tried the station, had a nice chat with one of the night crew, but no Cass. It was just as well. Impulsiveness never sat well with Cass.

She'd better go to bed. In the morning her mind would be clear, and she could get on with life. Demons always look mightier in the dark.

The next evening, Peyton hurried into her apartment building. She smiled at the manager on duty and headed towards the elevator.

"Excuse me, aren't you Ms. Adair?" the young man called.

"Yes," Peyton said. She stopped and turned toward his desk.

"A package arrived for you this afternoon. If you'll just sign for it . . ."

Peyton picked up the small box and shook it gently. It was from a small East Side gallery that dealt in glass and crystal sculpture. Peyton had been to a couple of openings there, but she'd never found anything she could afford.

"I can't figure out who it's from," she said. "Do you have a pair of scissors?"

The man handed her a heavy brass pair from his desk drawer. Carefully she slit the tape that held the wrapping in place and pulled out a tiny white box tied with a thin gold cord.

Peyton opened the box and lifted out a small glass pumpkin. It was heavy, substantial, delicately tinged with orange and green. Peyton searched for a card but found only the gallery's, with no hint of the giver.

"It's beautiful," the manager said. "How exciting; you have a secret admirer."

"Actually," Peyton said thoughtfully, "I may know who it's from. Thanks for holding it for me," she finished, returning the scissors. "See you later."

She sat that night in her rocker, cradling the glass pumpkin and listening to the tape of "On Air Columbus" over and over. It had to be from Cass. But what was he telling her? That he missed her? That he wanted her? That he cared?

His method troubled her. Although strong and so very private, Cass never beat around the bush when he had something to say. Subtlety was not his way. So why a glass pumpkin, to remind her of—

What? The painful truth that he couldn't love again? Cass wouldn't rekindle that memory; it was equally painful for him.

Had he come to some new revelation about himself that would focus their troubled relationship? And if so, why hadn't he come to tell her himself? Did he expect her to search him out and ask what he meant?

She had to be firm. She loved Cass, but she couldn't always be the one holding open the door. Any reconciliation—if that's what he wanted—had to be his idea. And it had to be in person.

Monday brought a shipment of Bremen Brats from Rainer's to her office. The station staff gobbled them down for lunch and teased her about her unknown admirer back in Columbus.

On Tuesday she received a blue stocking cap emblazoned with "Michigan" and a typed note telling her to "Keep your ears warm."

Wednesday brought a framed photograph of Old Man's Cave, the waterfall frozen in mid-tumble.

By Thursday Peyton's resolve was crumbling. When she arrived home that night, a bouquet of flowers awaited her in a WFKN mug, a riot of purple and magenta and green. She thanked the building manager and abruptly headed for the elevator.

What was Cass trying to do? All week he'd sent gifts that only reminded her of him, shared memories that she'd been trying to forget. If he was trying to be sure she wouldn't forget him, he was succeeding admirably. But why? He hadn't called, he had never signed a note or card.

Why was he dredging up bittersweet memories of a life gone by? She was here now, working and living in New York; she couldn't go back. Even if she wanted to. Even if he asked her to.

On Friday afternoon a courier delivered a cassette tape to Peyton's office. This one had a note in Cass's own bold handwriting: *Peyton: Please listen to this. C.S.*

Peyton nearly flew down the hall to a vacant studio and slammed the tape into a monitor. The theme music from "On Air Columbus" filled the control booth, then Cass's voice glided over her, smooth as velvet, "My guest tonight is Dr. Jane Thomas, who's here to talk about her new book, *The Intimacy Trap*."

She listened to the show again, the fifth or sixth time since Sally had sent it to her. Her heart thumped wildly as Cass defended the roles of intimacy and love in life.

Perhaps because she'd heard him repeating his challenges to Dr. Thomas so often, or perhaps because she wanted to so desperately, she suddenly believed him. He was speaking his own beliefs about love.

Cass *had* come to her through "On Air Columbus." Now it was up to her to go to him.

She called WFKN only to be told that Cass was out for the day, and frankly, the staff was glad. They hoped he'd stay gone for a couple of days so they could right their offices and get back to work.

Nor was Cass at home. The disembodied voice who worked at the answering service asked if she could take a message, but Peyton declined. If Cass were inaccessible by phone, she'd just have to see him in person.

Swiftly she made airline reservations and called her staff in.

"I'll be gone for a couple of days," she told them. "Here's what needs to be done." Rapidly she fired instructions, ticking off each person's name as she listed responsibilities. After informing Roger she would be out of town on personal business, she caught the subway home. Her flight left at seven; she had to pack quickly.

Two sharp raps at her door broke Peyton's concentration. Frowning, she tossed a last pair of underwear in her suitcase, snapped it shut and hoisted it to the floor.

She debated about not answering the knock. It had to be one of her neighbors; anyone else would have had to call upstairs to be buzzed in. Still, it would be good for one of them to know she'd be out of town so they could keep an eye on her apartment.

Determined to keep the conversation short, Peyton walked to the door. She flipped back the lock and swung the door open a few inches, catching it on the chain fastener.

A man, muffled in a scarf and overcoat, stood stuffing papers into an envelope.

"Yes?" Peyton said expectantly.

"Peyton?" came the familiar voice. "Can I talk to you?"

"Cass!"

FOURTEEN

Peyton fumbled with the chain and flung the door open.

"Come in!" she exclaimed. She could barely believe her eyes. All the anxiety and anticipation she'd reined in since her decision to fly to Columbus hit her with full force. She couldn't even catch her breath. He'd truly come to her!

Cass dropped his coat and scarf on a chair by the door and looked around. A slow, tiny smile tugged at his mouth when he saw the glass pumpkin on the coffee table. He seemed almost relieved, as if he'd been afraid that Peyton would have thrown away any reminder of him.

"I see you got it," he said, picking the pumpkin up and running his fingers around the smooth vertical ridges.

"All of them. The hat. The photo. The—" Her heart caught in her throat and she couldn't say more. Her pulse thundered in her ears and drove heat to her face. Unable to stand, she gestured to the sofa and dropped into her rocking chair.

Cass was looking at her closely, as if he were trying to discern what she made of his unexpected appearance. She mustn't seem too eager; that had driven him away before. But she couldn't help herself. Her body throbbed with warmth and need. Seeing Cass only reinforced how desperately she wanted him.

Cass sat down, but he kept watching her, cocking his head to view her from different angles. His scrutiny and the silence were unbearable. She had to know why he had come.

"Why are you here?"

"Actually, I have one more gift to deliver. And I thought you might think it was a cruel joke if I didn't do it in person." He handed her the envelope.

A love letter? How unlike Cass. But all of his behavior this week had been so unlikely that a letter seemed perfectly innocent. She slid her index finger under the flap and pulled out the contents.

A letter, but not the sort she'd been expecting. This one was notarized, on a letterhead she'd never seen before. Sloane-Adair Communications.

Quickly she scanned the letter, then let out a bewildered, throaty cry.

"This *is* a cruel joke," she whispered.

"It's no joke," Cass said. "Everything you just read is true."

"You're *giving* me half interest in WFKN?"

He nodded.

"Why?"

"You'd need a pretty good reason to leave New York. I thought this might be incentive enough."

"Why should I leave New York?" she asked cautiously. This was almost too good to be real. Her biggest dream—and Cass wanted to make it come true.

"I'd like to work with you again. Things at the station just aren't going smoothly without you. I didn't know how much I'd miss you until you were gone.''

''You want to work with me again,'' she repeated, her heart sinking.

So this was purely a business proposition. Only the last time they'd worked together, they'd ended up lovers. Was that the price of owning WFKN? Going back to Columbus as his mistress, with no promise of love, to be discarded when things got too close?

''Of course I want to work with you again.''

Peyton couldn't help herself; pain shook her voice and made her whole body tremble. ''That's all? Just happy little colleagues?''

''Of course not!'' Cass exclaimed. He watched the anger flash across Peyton's features, then he began to laugh.

''Then what?'' she snapped.

''Oh, Peyton, I'm sorry. Subtlety wasn't the answer, was it? Let me be plain. I love you. I just hope I'm not too late.''

''Wh-wh-what?''

Before she couldn't believe her eyes, but now she couldn't believe her ears. She must have wandered into some kind of fantasy dreamworld, where impossible things happened. If she looked around, she'd see clocks running backwards and pigs flying past her fourteenth story window. She could've sworn she'd heard Cass tell her he loved her!

And *that* couldn't be real! Soon she would wake up to the drab, cheerless gray of February. There would be no Cass to hug, only fleeting, fading memories to wrap around her.

Cass saw doubt clouding her face and acted swiftly. He would show her he was no illusion. Rising from the sofa, he pulled Peyton out of the rocking chair opposite and held her against his chest. Gently, he stroked her hair, smoothing down the unruly waves and shooting tiny jolts of electricity down her spine.

A dream couldn't feel so solid and genuine, so warm and safe. As Peyton relaxed, all thought of resistance fled. It was good to be back in Cass's arms again. It was right, natural. She belonged there.

If this was a dream, she didn't want to wake up.

"Peyton," Cass said softly in her ear, "I have three things to say. First, I'm sorry I hurt you. I had no idea how important you were to me, to becoming what I came home for. But when you left, I found out. I found out I needed you, that I needed your love. I found that I love you. And that I don't have to be afraid of repeating my mistakes, because I'm not the same man I was when I left New York. Because of you."

He kissed her hair tenderly.

"Second," he continued, "I want us to be together. I'd like it to be in Columbus, because there's where we found each other and because we have a business there. But Peyton," she felt him swallow hard, "if New York is home to you now, I'll come back here. The demons are gone."

He tilted her face upwards, gazed down into her eyes. The shadows were gone. His eyes were clear, the brilliant blue of the Caribbean sky. Hope planted a seed in Peyton's core.

"Katie's where she belongs—in a special place in my heart. But there's lots of extra room there—for you, and our family, for us. I can face anything with you."

"Cass, I—"

"Shh. Let me finish. Third, I want to marry you. I know it's sudden, and I'll wait as long as you want, but promise me you'll think about it. I want you to be my wife. I want to be your husband."

"Can I say something now?"

"Say 'yes,' " he pleaded.

"Cass, you came here out of the blue and sprang a lifetime's worth of surprises on me. Give me a minute to sort them all out!"

"Anything you want, sweetheart."

She rocked against him quietly, supported by his massive frame. Her mind flashed pictures of her and Cass together, the images she'd lain to rest last year. Newly resurrected, they danced in her brain with gleeful abandon.

Cass loved her!

He wanted to marry her!

He wanted to share his life and his work with her!

"Yes!" she murmured. "Oh yes!"

Cass moved his hand from her hair to her cheek and tilted her face towards his. Slowly, as if he had all the time in the world, he lowered his lips to hers.

His touch was magnetic; she couldn't have pulled away if she'd wanted to. He sealed their mouths together with moisture and heat, and Peyton reached up to pull his face closer to hers.

She would never get enough of him, never be able to fill her nights and days with too much of Cass. He was her other half, she his, and they'd found each other in spite of the pain and the hurt, or maybe because of it. But they were together, and Peyton was happy. So very happy.

She moved against his body, solid, sturdy, strong. He kissed her again, a deep, soul-filling kiss. He poured his emotions over her, bathing her in the love he'd almost forgotten how to share. She reached for him, gathered him in, and rocked him in the safe haven of her arms.

Cass's mouth roamed over her face, her neck, the

open collar of her blouse to the gentle swell of her breast. He showered her with kisses, warm and delicate as a spring rain. Gradually he became more demanding, heated, fierce. Peyton responded in kind; fever built in her blood.

She was burning for him. Internal fire scorched and crackled beneath her skin, and only Cass could cool her. She needed to feel him next to her, on top of her, his weight bearing down and leaving her breathless.

As if to oblige, Cass reached down to open her blouse and slide it off her shoulder. He smoothed his hands across her chest, tracing the outline of her collarbone, inching his way down to the weighty softness of her bosom.

Peyton abandoned herself to the sensation of him: his masculine scent; his lean hardness pressing against her; his deep, throaty groans filling the air around her. How had she imagined living without Cass? It didn't seem possible.

She swayed against him, dancing to a rhythm older than memory, younger than dawn. Cass moved with her in slow, sensuous motion, his own desire taut and hard against her. He guided her back to the bed and laid her sideways atop the bright floral comforter.

He lowered himself to her, and Peyton arched beneath him. She was hot, ready, aching for him to fill all the empty spaces inside her. She moaned and stretched her body to connect with Cass's full length. She wanted nothing but him touching her, nearer than her own flesh, pulsing with the combined force of pent-up need and sorrows released.

"Do you really love me?" she whispered, eager to hear the truth again.

"Like the sun," he murmured, grazing her belly with his lips. "Let me show you."

With a newfound urgency, he undressed her and shed his own clothing. Skirt, trousers, shirt and silky underthings landed in a jumbled heap by the bed; Cass's shorts decorated the top of the bookcase. And still he wasn't close enough to satisfy Peyton.

Eager, impatient with waiting, Peyton lifted herself to him and guided him deep within. Cass moved slowly at first, urging her to take her pleasure from him. Then, as they grew accustomed to one another, he increased the tempo. He brushed his chest over her softness, leaving behind faint patches of redness where his hair had been. Peyton clung to him, welcoming his size, scratching her nails gently along his back and buttocks.

The joy of it: union, completion. They had come so close to losing each other, that now they felt compelled to come together fiercely, passionately, nothing held in reserve. This was promise and fulfillment, expectation and commitment.

Peyton pulled him deeper, sensing the approaching climax of their lovemaking. She held him, aching, yearning, and then felt the ever-new wave of pleasure wash over her. It spiraled outward, over and through her, into Cass. With a hoarse cry, he joined her in release.

Pleasure, delight, satisfaction, trust. They'd swum in a sea of all four. They swam for a long time, buoyed by the wonder of love.

"What made you change your mind? Why did you come for me?" she asked much later.

"Life just lost its zest. I didn't have anyone to challenge me anymore. I couldn't even get 'On Air America' off the ground. Everywhere I was, everything I did, I kept looking for you.

"So you decided just like that?"

"No," he snorted. "I fought it for a long time. I probably knew the second week you were gone, but I couldn't admit it to myself. Then I dreamed about the church bells, and I knew I had to take a chance that you'd forgive me."

"The church bells?"

"I dreamed I was standing on a sidewalk, looking up at a church steeple. The bells were chiming, different tones for all the important events of my life. And when they got to you, they stopped. The bells wouldn't ring any more because I'd sent you away. And there was simply no reason to go on if I couldn't hear the bells."

"Your subconscious sounds like it was working overtime."

"Yeah." He paused, as if trying to decide whether to add anything to that short remark. "But the real kicker was when Katie showed up in my head. She told me I had to do something dramatic to get you back."

Slowly, cautiously, Cass told her about his last days with Katie: the trouble, the hurt, and finally, five years later, the hope and the release. The understanding that had freed him to come to her.

Peyton rolled to her side, curled up beside him. "So that's why you sent all those gifts. Something dramatic."

"I wanted to soften you up, get you ready for the grand gesture."

Peyton smiled. "You did that, all right. See the suitcase by the sofa? I just missed my flight to Columbus. I was going to make you explain this week to me!"

"Frankly, I didn't think you'd believe me if I just gave you half of WFKN. I had to prepare you for the idea a little."

"I still can't believe that. Sloane-Adair Communications," she said dreamily. "Are you sure you want to do that? You don't have to bribe me."

"It's not a bribe. I wanted to convince you that I'm serious about trusting you. I thought this might help you believe I can. We can start with the station and work it into the rest of our lives.

"But Peyton, I meant what I said. If you don't want to come back to Columbus now, I'll come to New York. We can do 'On Air America' from here."

"We?"

"Yes, we. I can't do it without you. You're the one who put together the right mix of shows that got the syndicates interested in the first place. If I didn't offer you the job before, it was because I was a big fool. I told myself that you should make your own decision about coming here, but really I was just trying to protect myself. Thank God I know better now."

"But if we stayed here, what about WFKN?"

"We could sell it or keep it as an investment, it doesn't matter to me. I just want us to be together."

"Sell WFKN?" she cried. "Not on your life! We're going back to run it the way it should be!"

"You don't mind? You just got here; this was a big move, a big career step. Not to mention that Roger will kill me."

"I'll handle Roger," she said firmly. "I've learned a lot here, but New York isn't home. It's too big, it's too cold, and it's too crazy. It's not the sort of place I want to bring up our family. Columbus is."

"So you'll come home?"

Home! Peyton smiled contentedly at the word. Then she frowned.

"What's the matter?"

"I just realized I don't have a home in Columbus."

Peyton furrowed her eyebrows. "My house sold a few weeks ago."

"You can always live with me," Cass squeezed her suggestively.

"Not a chance." She slapped his wrist playfully. "You offered me marriage—and I'm going to hold you to it."

"So marry me. Tomorrow. The day after. Then we can live together the right way." He dropped a kiss on her cheek. "The best way."

"What would you do if I said yes?"

"Go out and get a marriage license."

"So . . . you want to go get a marriage license tomorrow?"

"Seriously?"

"Seriously."

For once words failed Cass, but Peyton could see the delight and disbelief shining on his face. He pulled her tightly to him, conscious of how precious she was, marveling that she belonged to him.

"I love you," he whispered, closing his lips around one perfect earlobe.

"I love you, too. And we have the rest of our lives to prove it."

"At home."

"At home," she agreed, knowing that as long a they were together, they would always be home.

EPILOGUE

Dear Sal,

It was so good to hear from you last week. I'm excited that you and your partners have expanded again. Four stations! I'm in awe.

Cass and I talk all the time about expanding—goodness knows we've got enough talent working at 'FKN to manage a bigger operation. But you know, I'm really reluctant to take on too much while Katie's so young. Kids aren't little for very long; it doesn't seem fair to cheat them of their parents' time for those few years.

So 'FKN and "On Air America" are enough for now. But watch out when Katie's older. Sloane-Adair Communications will grow by leaps and bounds.

In the meantime, Katie's a joy. Cass is a born father, if you can imagine. Patient, fun, always ready to toss a softball or read a story. She keeps him toeing the line, though. Sometimes he complains that Katie inherited both her mom's and her namesake's stubborn streaks!

She helps me plan "Top Kid" and goes with me out on location when she's not too busy playing gardener. This year she planted radishes and cucumbers, and she's impatiently waiting for them to be ready to eat.

She's also impatiently waiting for something even bigger—a new little brother or sister. Yes, I'm pregnant, and the baby's due in October. I know I should have told you sooner, but we didn't want to tell anyone until we'd told Katie. Now she's threatening to boycott school this fall. "It takes too much time," she says. "I have to have time to play with Joey or Ellen." This from a kindergartner!

It's hard to believe it's been over six years since I left New York and you moved on from 'FKN. Look at us! I'm married to the man I was prepared to hate. We've got 1.5 kids (soon to be 2.0), and I'm living my dream of owning my own station.

And you . . . you've become a regular radio mogul, bouncing around the country with Jack and Andy, building that media "empire." And the twins have graduated from college! Sometimes I can't believe all the changes in our lives.

So much has happened. And yet it seems like yesterday that you were telling me that we have to take chances in life, and that love is worth all the risks—that it's the only thing that makes life worth living.

You know something? You were right. Thanks for teaching me that!

Love,
Peyton

SHARE THE FUN . . .
SHARE YOUR NEW-FOUND TREASURE!!

You don't want to let your new books out of your sight? That's okay. Your friends can get their own. Order below.

No. 120 HEART WAVES by Gloria Alvarez
Cass was intrigued by Peyton, one of the few who dared stand up to him.

No. 27 GOLDILOCKS by Judy Christenberry
David and Susan join forces and get tangled in their own web.

No. 28 SEASON OF THE HEART by Ann Hammond
Can Lane and Maggie's newfound feelings stand the test of time?

No. 29 FOSTER LOVE by Janis Reams Hudson
Morgan comes home to claim his children but Sarah claims his heart.

No. 30 REMEMBER THE NIGHT by Sally Falcon
Joanna throws caution to the wind. Is Nathan fantasy or reality?

No. 31 WINGS OF LOVE by Linda Windsor
Mac & Kelly soar to new heights of ecstasy. Are they ready?

No. 32 SWEET LAND OF LIBERTY by Ellen Kelly
Brock has a secret and Liberty's freedom could be in serious jeopardy!

No. 33 A TOUCH OF LOVE by Patricia Hagan
Kelly seeks peace and quiet and finds paradise in Mike's arms.

No. 34 NO EASY TASK by Chloe Summers
Hunter is wary when Doone delivers a package that will change his life.

No. 35 DIAMOND ON ICE by Lacey Dancer
Diana could melt even the coldest of hearts. Jason hasn't a chance.

No. 36 DADDY'S GIRL by Janice Kaiser
Slade wants more than Andrea is willing to give. Who wins?

No. 37 ROSES by Caitlin Randall
It's an inside job & K.C. helps Brett find more than the thief!

No. 38 HEARTS COLLIDE by Ann Patrick
Matthew finds big trouble and it's spelled P-a-u-l-a.

No. 39 QUINN'S INHERITANCE by Judi Lind
Gabe and Quinn share an inheritance and find an even greater fortune.

No. 40 CATCH A RISING STAR by Laura Phillips
Justin is seeking fame; Beth helps him find something more important.

No. 41 SPIDER'S WEB by Allie Jordan
Silvia's quiet life explodes when Fletcher shows up on her doorstep.

No. 42 TRUE COLORS by Dixie DuBois
Julian helps Nikki find herself again but will she have room for him?

No. 43 DUET by Patricia Collinge
Adam & Marina fit together like two perfect parts of a puzzle!

No. 44 DEADLY COINCIDENCE by Denise Richards
J.D.'s instincts tell him he's not wrong; Laurie's heart says trust him.

No. 45 PERSONAL BEST by Margaret Watson
Nick is a cynic; Tess, an optimist. Where does love fit in?

No. 46 ONE ON ONE by JoAnn Barbour
Vincent's no saint but Loie's attracted to the devil in him anyway.

No. 47 STERLING'S REASONS by Joey Light
Joe is running from his conscience; Sterling helps him find peace.

No. 48 SNOW SOUNDS by Heather Williams
In the quiet of the mountain, Tanner and Melaine find each other again.

No. 49 SUNLIGHT ON SHADOWS by Lacey Dancer
Matt and Miranda bring out the sunlight in each other's lives.

Meteor Publishing Corporation
Dept. 1292, P. O. Box 41820, Philadelphia, PA 19101-9828

Please send the books I've indicated below. Check or money order (U.S. Dollars only)—no cash, stamps or C.O.D.s (PA residents, add 6% sales tax). I am enclosing $2.95 plus 75¢ handling fee for *each* book ordered.

Total Amount Enclosed: $_____.

____ No. 120	____ No. 32	____ No. 38	____ No. 44
____ No. 27	____ No. 33	____ No. 39	____ No. 45
____ No. 28	____ No. 34	____ No. 40	____ No. 46
____ No. 29	____ No. 35	____ No. 41	____ No. 47
____ No. 30	____ No. 36	____ No. 42	____ No. 48
____ No. 31	____ No. 37	____ No. 43	____ No. 49

Please Print:

Name _____

Address _____ Apt. No. _____

City/State _____ Zip _____ •

Allow four to six weeks for delivery. Quantities limited.